MY BABY DADDY'S CRAZY NEW B**CH

A Dramatic Novel by Lady Lissa

PROLOGUE

Malayka

dropped my baby off at her father's house two days ago. I hadn't heard from Mackenzie or her father since that day I left her at his house. I cringed the days when I had to leave my little girl with her daddy. Not because Zion wasn't a good father; he was actually a great father. It's just that about eight months ago, he got himself a new girlfriend. I wasn't jealous of that bitch or nothing like that. But ever since she came into his life, shit had been nothing but chaos between my baby daddy and myself. What once was a very amicable co-parenting partnership between me and Zion, I now questioned leaving my child with him.

Three months ago, Mackenzie started coming home from her visits with bruises, scratch marks, and even a black eye once. When I brought it to Zion's attention, he always said had the same excuse; she's four and she played too hard. Bullshit! I had no doubt that my little girl played hard, but she didn't play that damn hard. It wasn't like she was clumsy or anything like that. She knew how to walk and stay on her feet. She was only four years old, so how hard did she play to get those big ass bruises on her back?

I suspected there was more going on in that house than I was being told. Of course, I asked Mackenzie how she got the bruises, but she could never give me a straight answer. She also had been crying a lot when it was her weekend to go visit her dad. She used to look forward to spending time with him, but now she didn't want to go. I wasn't sure what her reasons were, and no one seemed to want to give me a straight answer when I asked Zion and that hoodrat he was dating. But so help me God, if I found out that bitch Krystal had been putting her grimy hands on my baby girl, nothing would stop me from catching a charge. I'd beat that girl until she felt every ounce of pain she caused my child.

It was Zion's weekend and I had finally made my way to the nail spa. After a long work week, I definitely needed some pampering. I was sitting in the chair getting my toes and fingernails done when my phone started ringing. The woman who was doing my nails looked at me with an annoyed expression as I checked to see who was calling. I saw that it was Zion, so I pulled my fingers from the liquid and dried it as best I could on the towel as the lady worked on my other hand.

"Hey Zion, what's..." I didn't get to finish my question because as soon as I picked up the phone, I could hear Mackenzie screaming in the background. "What's going on? Why is Mackenzie screaming like that?"

"We're on our way to Texas Children's Hospital. Can you meet us there?" he asked, and it sounded as if he was out of breath.

I immediately pulled my hand and feet away from the two women at the salon and almost took off running without my shoes. "Texas Children's? What happened to my baby?"

"I'll explain everything when you get there! I have to go!" he said and hung the phone up. What the fuck? He couldn't just say some shit like that to me and hang the phone up.

"You have to pay!" the woman said frantically.

"Lady, my child is being taken to the hospital. I have to go!" I said as I stuck my feet in my shoes, wet toenails and all. At that moment, I didn't give two shits if I messed up my toes or shoes. My only concern was for my child as I hastily made my way to the exit.

The Asian woman ran to the door and stood in front of it, trying to block me from leaving. She must have been out of her fuckin' mind. Clearly, she didn't know how black people got down. "You have to pay... your feet, nails! You pay!"

I didn't bother answering her as I shoved her out of the way with all my might. My child was being taken to the hospital and this bitch was worrying about me paying for a service that hadn't been completed. She definitely had me fucked all the way up. If that bitch didn't understand what I was going through right now, then she had a fucking problem. There was no way I wasn't going to stop whatever I was doing to go see about my baby girl.

As I charged out the door, I rushed to get in my car. I hopped in and peeled out of the parking lot. I put my emergency lights on because I was going to break every speed limit to get there. I prayed that I wouldn't get pulled over by the police on my way to the hospital.

The whole time I was driving, I kept hoping that her injuries weren't too bad. I started praying as I drove like a bat outta hell. "God, if you can hear me right now, please let my baby be okay. Please cover her in your blood, Lord and take away her pain. Please Lord, I beg of you to help my child through whatever she's going through. Amen," I said, but then I had an afterthought. "And Lord, if that bitch had something to do with my child getting hurt, please allow me to get a good lawyer cuz I'm gon' need one to beat the murder charge."

When I pulled into the hospital parking lot, I wasted no time rushing inside. I ran up to the front desk and said, "My name is Malayka Hughes. My daughter Mackenzie was brought here by her father. Where are they?"

The woman looked at me and asked, "What did you say your daughter's name was?"

"Mackenzie Harris, her father's name is Zion Harris!"

"Yes ma'am, they just got here a couple of minutes ago. The doctor will be with them shortly."

"Where are they?" I asked.

"I'm sorry ma'am, but only two people are allowed in the room with the child."

"Well, I'm her mother, so whoever else is in that room needs to get the fuck out now!" I said as I rushed through the back doors.

"Ma'am, you can't just go back there!" the woman said as she followed behind me. I listened for my daughter's cries and followed my way toward the exam room.

When I finally found the room, I busted in to find my baby screaming at the top of her lungs and a doctor examining her arm that appeared to be bent out of shape. "Ma'am, you cannot be in here! Only two people..."

"I'M HER MOTHER!" I said as I casted my gaze at that crazy bitch, Krystal. I rushed over to her and got in her face. "If you had anything to do with this, I swear I will kill you!"

"That's some big words coming from someone who can't fight," she said as she smiled evilly at me.

"Oh, believe what you want to. When it comes to my child, you'd be surprised the lengths I'd go through to protect her. If I find out you had anything to do with this, you don't have to worry about me fighting you. Like I said before, I will kill you."

Zion got between us and said, "Malayka calm down!"

"Calm down?! You want me to calm down? Our daughter is laying there with what looks like a broken arm. I know that bitch had something to do with it!" I said.

"I'm going to need you all to calm down!" the doctor stated. "I need only the parents of the patient in the room."

Zion turned to his bitch and said, "Baby, wait for me in the lobby please."

She looked pissed but what the hell was she going to do? She had no choice but to get the fuck out. As she made her way toward the door, I watched her and my baby girl exchange looks. The look that my daughter had on her face was a look of fright. That scared look in my baby's eyes was all I needed to see to let me know what I already suspected. That bitch had something to do with whatever happened to my little girl.

She was the reason my baby was in this hospital. I guess the doctor must have given Mackenzie a sedative because soon after Krystal left the room, she fell asleep.

Since the very first time I met that bitch, I told Zion that she was trouble. From the moment I laid eyes on her, I knew I was going to have problems with her. I didn't know that I'd want to kill her, but I did. And trust me, if I found out that she broke my child's arm, she would have hell to pay. Believe that!

CHAPTER ONE

Malayka

When I met Zion Harris, I fell head over heels immediately. I knew from the moment I laid eyes on him that I'd be with him forever. He hadn't even opened his mouth yet, so imagine how I melted when he did open his mouth to speak. It wasn't that I was weak or anything like that. It's just that my palms began to sweat, I felt a little lightheaded, and my heart was pounding so hard I thought it would pop right out of my chest.

He was absolutely the most handsome man I had ever met before. He was standing in the line for the pharmacy as I prepared prescriptions for customers. No, I wasn't the pharmacist. I was a pharmaceutical tech studying to become a pharmacist. I had big dreams of doing all I could do so that when I decided to have children, I could give them the best life I could. I just happened to look up and into Zion's eyes. It was almost as if he was hypnotizing me with his eyes.

He stood there in a suit, but he still looked hot. Suit or no suit, I could tell he worked out. I wouldn't mind him working out with me sometime, and I wasn't talking about in a gym either.

"Malayka, please pay attention to what you're doing. I'm sure that script doesn't say fill the bottle to capacity..." Nina, the pharmacist said in a hushed tone.

I looked to see what she was talking about and saw that I had filled a huge bottle to the top with those huge horse pill antibiotics. The prescription was only for 90 pills, but I had gone over that amount.

"Sorry Nina," I said with a smile as I placed the pills back on the pallet and began to count them out again.

I needed to get my ass to that counter, so I counted those pills by five, so I could finish quicker. When I was done, I capped the bottle and placed it in the bag. By the time it was Zion's turn, I was waiting to help him.

"Good afternoon," I smiled my brightest smile. "Are you picking up or dropping off?"

"Dropping off," he said as he handed me a prescription.

I put the information in and looked back up into his grey eyes. "Are you Zion?"

"Yes."

"Is your number still 713-459-6782?"

"Yes."

"Okay, we can have that prescription ready for you in less than 10 minutes," I said.

"Wow! That fast, huh?"

"Yep, I'm going to handle this one personally," I said.

"Oh, so you're the pharmacist?"

"Not yet, but it won't be long now. I'm actually doing my clinicals here." I hoped what I said impressed him as much as his looks impressed me.

He looked to be 6'2, with a bald head that shined like a disco ball, pretty teeth, a chiseled chin covered with a goatee, and beautiful rich caramel skin. As he smiled at me, I felt my lips becoming dry as the cotton sensation took over my mouth, draining it of all moisture.

"Are you going to wait for your prescription or come back?" I asked.

"Well, if you can have it ready in 10 minutes, I'll sit here and wait."

"Okay great! Just give me a few minutes."

As he took a seat, I took the prescription and began working on it immediately.

"What are you doing?" Nina asked.

"Filling a prescription. What's it look like?"

"You're supposed to go in the order they're received."

"Oh, c'mon Nina. You can't tell me that you've never bumped a prescription to the top of the line before..." I said as I waited for her to deny it. "Exactly!"

"So, what's going to happen when those people who've already been waiting 10 or 15 minutes sees him get his prescription first?" she asked with a smug look on her face.

"I'll cross that bridge when I get to it," I informed her.

I looked at the prescription for Amoxicillin and filled it quickly. I printed the label, attached it to the bottle, and slipped it inside the bag. I made my way back to the counter and looked at Zion. He hopped up and approached the counter.

"Already?" he asked with a surprised expression.

"I told you I was fast."

"That you are, Ma-lay-ka!" he said as he read my name badge. "That's a pretty name."

"Thanks. I like yours too."

I tallied his total, he paid the copay for it, and I handed him the bag. "Enjoy the rest of your day," I said with a smile.

"You too beautiful," he said, which caused me to blush like a teenager.

He left the counter and then all hell broke loose. "Excuse me, I've been waiting for my prescription for the past 20 minutes!" a woman said.

"I've been waiting on medication for my little boy for the past 15 minutes!" a man shouted out. "All I wanna know is how dude come in after us but left before us! Where the hell is my son's medication, lady?!"

I looked over at Nina who had the 'I told you so' expression on her face and tried to calm the customers down. "I'm sorry you've all been waiting so long. I promise to get right on your orders and have them filled in just a couple of minutes," I said.

"That's some straight bullshit!" the man fumed.

I didn't even bother to answer as I walked away from the counter to get their prescription orders filled. As soon as I stood next to Nina, she whispered, "I told you. You can't play that here boo."

"Shit, I know now," I said.

Thanks to Nina, we managed to fill the orders and get them to the customers, along with a five-dollar gift card for their inconvenience. I promised myself and Nina that I'd never do anything like that again.

That evening, I did something I had never done before. After Zion left, I went back in his account and wrote down his number. I couldn't help it because I couldn't get that man out of my mind. When I got home, I took a shower, ate a salad, and then got comfortable. As I sat down on the sofa, I pulled out my phone and the receipt paper with Zion's number on it and gave him a call. I mean, why not? I didn't have anything to lose. I just hoped that he wasn't in a relationship or anything like that because then that would be embarrassing.

I took a deep breath and punched the numbers in the phone. As the phone rang, I contemplated hanging up because this man didn't know me. What if he went off on me for getting his number? What if he reported me for calling him? I was about to hit the end button when he picked up.

"Hello," he answered. The sound of his voice made me melt like butter on my sofa cushions.

"Hello, is this Zion?"

"Yes, who's this?"

"Um, it's Malayka..."

"Malayka? From the pharmacy?" he asked.

"Yes..."

"Did I forget something?"

"No... it has nothing to do with your visit today."

"Then I'm confused as to why you're calling me."

"I'm sorry. It's just that once you left, I couldn't stop thinking about you. I know it's out of line and a little unorthodox for me to go through these measures to speak to you, but I couldn't help it. If you would like me to not call you again, I can hang up now, and I'll never bother you again," I said. I mean, I didn't know what else to say. I felt like a kid in school being reprimanded by the teacher for cutting up.

"No, it's fine. I'm just surprised to hear from you, that's all. What made you call me?"

"Like I said, I couldn't stop thinking about you ever since you left. I just would like to get to know you better, unless you're already involved with someone," I quickly said.

"No, I just happen to be a single man at the moment," he said.

"Great! So, are you open to making a new friend?"

"Definitely. I like your brazen attitude already. Most chicks are afraid to go after what they want."

"Thanks. I just felt like we had some kind of connection, ya know?"

"Uh, okay," he said as if he didn't feel the same. I couldn't expect him to though. I mean, we did just meet, and men were sometimes slow about getting their feelings together.

"So, maybe we could go out this weekend, if you aren't busy."

Long story short, we went out that weekend and had been together ever since. I think my relationship with Zion would've lasted longer if I hadn't gotten pregnant within the first four months. Our relationship was so new a pregnancy was the last thing on our minds. I'm not even sure how I got pregnant because we had been so careful. When I found out that I was having a baby, I didn't know if I should talk to Zion about it or head to the nearest clinic to terminate it.

I couldn't terminate the pregnancy if I wanted to. I was already in love with being a mommy. As I rubbed my hand over my belly bump, I wondered when would be a good time to break the news to Zion. This news was so unexpected for me, so I knew he wasn't expecting it. My nerves grew worst as I picked up the phone to call Zion. My fingers trembled as I hit the send button to make the call.

"Hey babe," he answered in his usual upbeat voice.

"Hey, are you busy?"

"A little, why? What's going on?"

"Well, I was just wondering if we could meet for dinner tonight."

"I thought you had to work tomorrow morning."

Usually, we didn't see each other when I had to work the next morning because we didn't get to sleep until the wee hours of the morning. The last thing I wanted was to go to work all tired and have to deal with grumpy customers. For that reason, we only got together when I was off the next day or had to work in the afternoon.

"I do, but there's something I need to discuss with you. It's kind of important," I said.

"Okay. Do you want me to come over to your place, or you wanna meet somewhere?"

"We can meet at my place, if that's okay."

"Yea sure. I'll see you when I get off," he said.

"Okay great!" I was about to hang up but wanted to end things on a good note. "Zion?"

"Yea?"

"I love you."

"I love you too, bae," he said as we ended the call. I couldn't help but smile at that. He actually did love me, and I loved him. With that being said, I knew that the two of us would find a way to make this work for our baby. The rest of my day went by smoothly, but when it was time for me to clock out, I got nervous all over again. On the drive home, I had to give myself a pep talk.

"Malayka, you can do this. I mean, he said he loves you, so what can go wrong?"

I decided to pick up dinner from Chili's on the way home. There was no way I could stand in the kitchen and cook a meal as nervous as I was. My stomach was in knots but fluttering like I had butterflies dancing inside. I didn't know how I was supposed to feel right now. I was nervous, but I was happy. I loved Zion and we made the perfect couple. I knew from watching him with his niece that he'd make a great father someday. I had no idea someday would come so soon.

I pulled into the driveway and set the food on plates. I put them on a baking sheet and put the pan in the warm oven. I wanted to keep the food warm and fresh for when Zion arrived. He finally rang the bell ten minutes later. I opened the door and we embraced as he kissed my lips.

"How was your day?" he asked.

"It was good. How about yours?"

"It was fine." He stared at me intently as he spoke those words. I was so nervous, and I just knew that my face must've betrayed me. His next question confirmed my facial expression. "So, what's going on with you? You seem to have something weighing on your mind." Dammit! I was hoping to wait until after dinner to tell him that we were going to become parents, but I guess now was as good a time as any.

"I thought we'd eat first and then have a conversation, but..."

"What's going on? You're starting to make me nervous," he said.

"I'm sorry about making you nervous, but at least your feelings match mine."

He took my hands in his and pulled me toward the sofa. We sat on the sofa facing each other as he continued to look into my eyes. "What's going on? You know you can talk to me about anything."

"I'm pregnant!" I blurted before I lost the courage to do so this evening.

"You're pregnant?" he asked as he took a deep gulp. He ran his hand down his face as his face took on an ashen color. He looked like he was sick, literally.

"Yea."

"Wow!"

"Are you upset?" I asked, hoping that he'd say no. I wanted him to tell me that he was thrilled we were having a baby. However, I didn't want him to tell me what he thought I wanted to hear. I wanted him to be honest with me no matter how he felt. I never wanted Zion to feel as if he couldn't tell me the truth because of how I'd react. If we loved each other, we could get through anything, right?

"I'm not upset. Shocked would be a better word," he said. "Are you sure the test is right?"

"Well, they say the home tests are pretty accurate. I was going to make a doctor's appointment to confirm it in a couple of weeks though," I said.

"A couple of weeks?" he asked as he stood up while scratching his head.

"Yea..."

"I think you should go tomorrow."

"Tomorrow? I have to work in the morning," I said.

"Then go in the afternoon. I think we need to get this finalized so we can know how to proceed," he said.

"What do you mean so we can know how to proceed?"

"Babe, we've only been dating for a little while. We need to make some decisions if you really are pregnant."

"What kind of decisions are you needing to make? This is my pregnancy and my body..."

"But my child!"

"OUR CHILD!" I said. I could feel myself growing frustrated. This wasn't how I expected things to turn out. I imagined us embracing and making love, then talking about our future plans while we ate dinner. This argument right here... totally unexpected.

"Right, which is why we should make these decisions together!"

"Zion, I love you and I love this child already. I don't need to go to the doctor for them to confirm this pregnancy..."

"What? Why not?"

I lifted my shirt to show him the small bump that had started developing. It's funny how I never noticed it before I found out that I was pregnant. It was like as soon as I found out, I placed my hand on my belly and the bump was there. I told Zion I was going to go to the doctor in a couple of weeks to find out for sure whether I was pregnant or not, but that wasn't the exact truth. The only reason I was going to the doctor was to find out my due date. As I watched the expression on his face as he stared at my belly, his expression had me more confused than ever.

"So, you knew you were pregnant for a while and you're just telling me now? Why would you keep something this important from me?" he asked as he glared at me. Yea, he was clearly angry right now. I couldn't believe he was accusing me of hiding my pregnancy from him. I was very hurt by his insinuation, but his next words cut way deeper than the other ones. "Did you plan to trap me with a kid all along?"

As I fought back the tears that threatened to fall, I forced myself to speak. I could not believe things between us had gone this far. "TRAP YOU? YOU THINK I GOT PREGNANT ON PURPOSE?!" I yelled.

"Well, I've been using condoms, so you tell me," he said.

"You aren't even making any sense right now. We have been cautious with that except..."

"Except what?"

"Except that one time..." I let the words trail off as I thought about that time we were so horny we forgot about a condom. It was actually the second time we had sex.

I watched as he seemed to be in deep thought, probably thinking about how that time happened. He hadn't even been thinking about using a condom that night. I had thought to tell him something but didn't wanna ruin the mood by having him stop to put one on. I just didn't think I'd get pregnant because he didn't use it that one time. Of course, I knew it was possible. I just didn't think it would happen to me. If that was the time I conceived, I was about four months along already.

"I gotta get out of here," he said as he made his way toward the front door.

"So... so... so, you're just gonna walk out on me?" I asked as the tears I had been holding back finally started to fall.

"I wasn't expecting to hear this shit Malayka! I just need some time to think about things!"

"Why is it that guys always needed time to prepare themselves? I'm carrying the baby and I don't even have that luxury! I wasn't trying to trap you Zion. That night, we both forgot about using protection, so you can't put that all on me like I was the one who did you wrong. I didn't do anything wrong," I said as I stood there crying like a baby.

Zion turned to look at me and I could see that he was conflicted with his emotions. He walked over to me and wrapped me in his arms. I held onto him really tight as I continued to cry. I didn't want to be a single parent. I was in a loving relationship with my boyfriend. I had hopes that we would get through this as an engaged couple or something, but I certainly didn't see him walking out on me.

"Just give me some time to digest this, okay?" he said as he kissed my forehead and released me.

"But..."

"Just give me some time..." With that being said, he turned his back and walked out the door. I wrapped my arms around myself and cried as I slid down the length of the door until my butt touched the floor. I wrapped my arms around my knees and cried as my heart shattered into tiny pieces.

I could not believe any of that had happened. After a few minutes, I remembered the dinner plates that were in the oven on warm. I went into the kitchen and pulled them out. I didn't know what else to do, so I picked up the phone and called my sister. I didn't wanna be alone right now.

"Hey sissy..." she answered in her bubbly tone.

"Brianna..."

"Oh my God! What's wrong?"

"Can you come over?" I asked as I sniffled.

"I'm on my way," she said as she ended the call.

15 minutes later, she was knocking on my door. My sister and I were really close, and we were close with our mom. I knew that she would show up when I told her I needed her. That was just the way we were. Whenever we needed each other, including our mother, we all dropped everything to be there. Our father had walked out on our mom when Brianna was a baby. He was one of those dudes that said he was going for cigarettes and never came back. From what my mom told us, she was devastated, but still loved him. So, when she ran into him a year later, all those feelings that she had for him resurfaced and they fell in bed again.

When she told him that she was pregnant with me, he didn't even wait for my mom to give birth. He left when she was seven months pregnant and never came back. My mom ran into him again years later, but she didn't even try to speak to him that time. I never knew why my dad didn't want to be with my mom. I didn't know why he just walked out on his children. I just prayed that things would be different when I got pregnant. But judging by the way Zion just walked out on me it seemed as if the cycle would be repeating itself. I hated the thought of being a single mother. That wasn't what I wanted, especially knowing how hard my mom struggled to raise me and my sister.

I opened the door and she took one look at me and held her arms out. I walked into them and began to cry again. "What's wrong? What happened?"

"Zion walked out on me," I sobbed.

"What? Why?"

She led me to the sofa and once we sat down, she asked, "What happened? I thought you guys were happy."

"We were..." I said as I continued to sob.

"Well, what happened?"

"I told him I was pregnant, and he just walked out on me."

"What? You're pregnant? Why didn't you tell me?" she asked.

"I just found out myself." I said.

"Wow! I can't believe he just walked out on you. What'd he say when he left?"

"He said he just needed some time."

"TIME?! REALLY?!" she fussed. "Why do men always say that bullshit when a woman tells them she's pregnant? What the hell does he need time for? He ain't the one carrying the baby!"

"I don't know. I still have a hard time believing that he just left me like that." She pulled out her phone and unlocked it. "Wait... what are you doing?"

"I'm going to call him. He has some explaining to do about that shit!"

"No wait!"

"Wait for what?"

"Don't call him. You might just make things worse," I said.

The last thing I needed was for my sister to call my man about my pregnancy. He didn't need to be hounded by her. If anyone needed to call him, it should be me. But since he asked me for some time, I was going to let him have that. I didn't think it would be a good idea for VaBrianna to call Zion, at least not right now. Now, if he didn't come around within the next week or so, I'd definitely be giving him a call.

"What? How can things get worse than him walking out on you? That won't solve anything. He needs to march his ass back over here so the two of you can talk this out," she said.

While I agreed with her about that, I still didn't think she needed to make a phone call to him. He didn't even know I had asked her to come over. I didn't want him to think that I needed my sister to speak on my behalf.

"I know, but if he needs some time, I have to give it to him."

"That's only going to make things worse for your situation. If you think giving him time is what he needs to come around, you're wrong. You need to demand that he come over..."

"I'm not doing that Brianna."

"But you need to..."

"BRIANNA!" She immediately stopped talking as she stood there with her lips pursed together in a tight line. "I need you to listen to me. It's my baby and my relationship we're talking about. I'm just going to give him some time to think things through. He'll come around in a couple of days."

"Okay. I'll let it go, but you're wrong if you think he's gonna come around in a couple of days. You're giving him too much freedom, and that's only going to make him run. I bet he thinks you got pregnant on purpose to try and trap him like he's worth trapping."

Even though she was right about that, I didn't confirm it. In my heart, I really believed that Zion would be back in a few days, profess his love for me, and rejoice about my pregnancy. Of course, that was all a part of my fantasy. Things never happened like that in real life, only in the movies. Even in the movies, teen girls who got pregnant had their little boyfriends stand by them. Not in real life. At least not in my real life.

I wished I had grabbed the bull by the horns and forced Zion to deal with my pregnancy the way my sister told me to. Maybe if I had done that, our relationship might've had a different outcome.

CHAPTER TWO

Zion

When I agreed to go over to Malayka's house this evening, the last thing I expected was to get news about a pregnancy. I thought I'd go over, we'd have dinner, and then finish things off in the bedroom. Shit, we hadn't even gotten to the food before she busted my bubble about the evening. As I sat in the line at Checkers, my mine replayed itself to her telling me she was pregnant.

"Dammit!" I said as I smacked my steering wheel.

I couldn't believe what could have been a great evening had turned into something so terrible. I cared a lot about Malayka, but a pregnancy wasn't something I bargained for so soon. I would've never used protection if I wanted to have a baby with her. We had only been dating a few months. I could tell that she was looking for us to ride off into the sunset and be happy, but that wasn't how I felt. I was in absolute shock at hearing this news.

I thought about calling her, but I couldn't. I didn't wanna call and smooth things over just yet. How could she have gotten pregnant when we were using condoms? Condoms were supposed to keep the woman from getting pregnant. I knew there was always that one percent that shit could happen, but I never thought I'd be part of that percentage.

I got my food from the drive-thru and headed home. I hit the call button on my phone and my brother's phone began to ring. "Hey bro man, wassup with you?"

"Hey Nate, what's up with you?"

"Chillin'. Whatchu got going on?"

"I'm on my way, but I found out something a lil while ago that got me buggin'."

"Oh yea? What'd you find out? Did you lose all your money you had in the stock?"

"Nah, nothing like that."

15

"Then what is it man? Sounds like you got a lot on your mind," he said.

"Hell yea! I just left Malayka's place," I began.

"Malayka? Is that the chick you been messing with lately?"

"Yea, remember I told you I met this chick at the pharmacy a few months back? The chick that got my number from the store's computer and called me up?"

"Yea, the bold chick..."

"Yea, that one."

"Okay, so what's the problem? She break up with you?"

"Nah, she told me that she's pregnant."

"Whaaaaat?! My lil bro about to be a daddy! Congrats man!" Nate said in an excited tone.

"Nah, no congrats necessary man."

"What? The kid ain't yours? Ol' girl was cheating on you?"

"Nah bro, nothing like that. The kid is mine..."

"Well, congrats man!!"

"Dude stop with the congrats already!"

"What's wrong? You just said your girl is having your baby. Congratulations should be necessary, right?" he asked. I could tell from the sound of his voice that he was confused. I didn't mean to confuse him. I just didn't know what was the point of having him congratulate me when I wasn't sure how I felt about this kid.

"Look, I ain't ready to be nobody's daddy. We only been dating a few months. We not living together, engaged, nothing..."

"Aye, if that's your kid, you have to step up."

"But..."

"No buts dude. You remember how mom told us she felt when dad left her?"

"Yea..."

"You can't do that to your kid, bro. That's your blood running through that kid's veins. He or she will be your responsibility and you owe it to that chick to be the man our ol' man wasn't."

"Dude..."

"Dude nothing, bruh! If I had a chick pregnant, nothing would keep me from being a daddy to that kid. Any nigga can father a kid, but it takes a real man to step up and be the daddy. You remember that shit when you think about walking out on that baby and his mom. Think about how mom felt when she told us the story about why we didn't have a dad like our friends did. Do you want your seed going through that shit?"

He brought up some valid points, but I still wasn't ready to be a dad. "I hear ya bro. I guess it was just a shock." I said what he wanted me to say. I didn't know what I was going to do. I knew one thing though... I was going to take all the time I needed to get my mind right. "Aye, thanks for the talk. I'ma holla atchu later."

"Aight. Make mama proud Zion. She ain't raised us by herself so we could turn into our father," he said.

"I gotchu," I said as I ended the call.

I wasn't sure how I was going to deal with the news that Malayka had given me this evening. I was just gonna sleep on it and hope I make the right decision the next time I spoke to her. One thing was for sure... I wasn't making any hasty decisions to please anyone.

A week later, my mom hit me up. I wasn't surprised because my mom and I spoke at least once or twice a week. I was surprised when she brought up me becoming a father. I hadn't expected my brother to contact my mom about that shit, especially since I should've been the one to tell her.

"Hey ma," I answered.

"Hey baby, how are you doing?" she asked.

"I'm handling life. How bout you?"

"I'm okay, but I'm a little upset with you."

"You're upset with me? What'd I do?"

"How come you didn't tell me I was going to be a Gigi?" she asked.

"A what? Come again," I said. I was confused as hell. What the fuck is a Gigi?

"Why weren't you the one to tell me that I was going to be a grandmother?"

Fuck! I shouted to myself once what she said had settled in my brain. I hadn't told my mom anything about the baby because I hadn't spoken to Malayka since she broke the news to me. I was going to kill my brother for telling my mom the news before I did.

"Who told you that?" I asked, even though I already knew who had spilled the beans.

"Nate told me, but I'ma ask again, why didn't you tell me? You know how much I love babies!" she gushed.

"I'm sorry I didn't tell you mom. I'm still trying to process the news myself," I admitted.

"What do you mean by that? If a woman tells you she's pregnant and you know the baby is yours, what is there to process?"

"I don't know mom. I mean, me and Malayka ain't been together but a few months..."

"What you saying? You think she cheated on you?"

"No ma'am. I know she didn't cheat on me," I said. I wasn't going to make Malayka look worse than she was. She was a cool chick and the mother of my child. I didn't want my mom thinking any less of her.

"Well, if she didn't cheat on you and you know the baby is yours, then you need to take care of your responsibilities as that baby's father!"

"You talking like the baby is here already. The baby ain't even born yet," I said.

"I'ma need you to come over here when you get a chance."

"What for?"

"Do I need a reason to get my son over here?" she asked in a sterner tone.

"No ma'am. I'll come by after work," I stated.

"Good, I'll be waiting on you and don't think you can give me some bullshit excuse about why you couldn't make it either."

I knew better than to mess with my mom. If she said she wanted to see me, I already knew that I needed to show up or I'd have hell to pay. "I'll be there mom," I said as we ended the call. I immediately called my brother as soon as I got off the phone with my mom.

"What up baby boy?" he asked all jolly and shit.

"Aye, did you tell mom that Malayka was pregnant?" I decided to get right down to the point of my phone call and skip the pleasantries. There was no sense in beating around the bush because I was upset enough already. He was quiet for a few minutes, so I went in. "What the hell did you tell her that shit for, bro? I mean, it wasn't for you to say."

"I know, and I didn't mean for that to happen. What had happened was..."

"What happened was you told my damn business! You had no right to do that shit, yo."

"I wasn't trying to tell yo business on purpose, bro. I promise. I just assumed you had already told her. I didn't know she didn't know until after I said something," he said. "I'm sorry bro."

"Yea, but now mom wants me to come over tonight and you know she bout to preach."

"Well, if you still unsure about how you feel concerning that baby, she needs to talk to you. You know mom don't wanna hear nothing but you telling her when the baby coming. I'm sorry that I told her before you, but if it helps you make the right decisions pertaining to your kid, I'm glad."

"Yea, you say that shit because you ain't in my shoes..."

"Nigga, if I were having a kid with a chick that loved me, I'd embrace that shit. Hell, I'm still out here looking for the right one. You already found her and she's giving you something no other bitch can ever give you..."

18

"Which is what exactly?" I asked as I twisted up my lips.

"Your first kid, bro. She's giving you your firstborn seed."

"Yea, aight. Well, I gotta go. I'm holla at you later."

"Aight bro. Love you man," he said.

"I love you too bro."

The rest of the afternoon at work had me on edge. I was nervous about seeing my mom because I knew she was going to do just like my brother... talk about her struggles to raise us as a single parent. I dreaded that talk. I had no idea what I was in for though. My mom is something else.

I thought about calling Malayka to see how she was doing and to ask about her doctor's appointment. I decided I would do that once I left my mom's house. She and I had some decisions to make and I could no longer ignore that fact. Whether I was ready to be a dad or not, it was happening. I also decided I didn't want to pursue a relationship with Malayka anymore. I cared about her a lot but the stress from this pregnancy was just too much. If this had happened two years down the line, I think I would've been more excited about becoming a parent with her.

I pulled into my mom's driveway and took a deep breath before walking in the house. I prayed that she would just listen to my side of things before she ripped my head off. I knew she wouldn't be happy about the way I had been treating Malayka. Hell, I wasn't happy with my actions either. I just didn't know how to make things better between us.

"Ma! Where you at?" I asked as I walked toward the kitchen. I could smell the sweetest aromas coming from there and knew she had to be in the kitchen. Just as I suspected, she was taking a cobbler out of the oven.

"Hey son, I thought for a moment that you had changed your mind about coming over," she said as she kissed my cheek and returned my hug.

"I wouldn't do that mom. I knew how important it was for us to have this conversation."

"You're right." She turned the oven off and asked, "Are you hungry? I made a meatloaf earlier since I knew you were coming."

"I sure am," I said.

"Well, why don't you go wash up and I'll make you a plate?" she suggested. On my way to the bathroom, I heard a knock on the door. I assumed it was my brother, but wondered why he was knocking instead of just walking in. I didn't waste much time worrying about it because if it was him, I'd just see him when I went back to the kitchen.

However, I almost shitted on myself when I saw Malayka sitting at the dining room table once I returned to the kitchen. I swallowed hard as I averted my eyes from hers and looked to my mom for answers. I had introduced her to Malayka once and that was because I had gone with her to the pharmacy to get a prescription filled. I really wasn't expecting to be ambushed by the two of them today.

"Hey Zion," Malayka said.

"Hey, what are you doing here?" I asked.

"I invited her," my mom said.

"Why would you do that? I thought this little meeting was between you and me."

"Well, at first I thought that too, but then I decided to involve this young lady. I wasn't sure how to reach her, so I called the pharmacy and was glad when I found out she was working today. I told her who I was and invited her to join us. Do you have a problem with that?"

"No ma'am. I'm just shocked, that's all," I said. What else was I going to say?

"Malayka, would you like something to eat honey? I made meatloaf, mashed potatoes, and green beans," my mom announced.

"Oh, no thank you..."

"What do you mean no? I know you're just getting off from work, so you must be hungry. You're carrying my grandchild, so you need to eat for him or her too. You're not eating for just yourself anymore," mom said.

"Yes ma'am, I know. It's just that I'm a little nervous about being here..."

"There's no need to be nervous. We're family now. Go wash up and I'll make you a plate. The bathroom is the second door on the right."

"Yes ma'am," Malayka said as she stood up. She walked by me and headed to the bathroom.

I walked over to my mom and whispered, "How come you didn't mention inviting her when we spoke earlier?"

"I didn't decide to invite her until a couple of hours ago. I thought it would be a good idea to bring the two of you together, especially since Nate said you were having a hard time accepting the fact that she's pregnant. You know I raised you better than that," she whispered back through clenched teeth.

I was going to kill my brother, for sure.

CHAPTER THREE

Malayka

I hadn't heard from Zion since I announced my pregnancy to him a week ago. I wanted to call him but decided against it so many times. What would be the point of reaching out to him when he asked for space? What if he was still confused about his feelings for me? What if he wasn't sure how he felt about my pregnancy? What if he wanted me to terminate my pregnancy? I hoped that wasn't the case because I had already gone to the doctor and according to her, my baby was due in 21 weeks. That didn't leave us with much time to prepare, but one thing was for sure... terminating this pregnancy was out of the question.

I prayed that Zion would come around and do the right thing for our child. Growing up without a father really fucked me up. It made me feel like I wasn't good enough for my dad to love me. My mom showered me and my sister with love, but it hurt to see my friends with their dads in their lives and I had none. I promised myself that if ever I had a baby, I'd make sure that I was married to the father first. That's one promise that I failed to come through with for my child.

My child wasn't even born yet, and I had failed as a parent already. When I was told that I had a phone call at work today, I thought it might be Zion. Imagine my surprise when I picked up the call and it was his mother instead. I didn't know why she was calling, especially since I hadn't heard from her son.

"Hello," I answered the call.

"Is this Malayka?"

"Yes, who's this?"

"This is Loretta Harris, Zion's mother. I believe you're dating my son. Am I right?"

I swallowed hard because I wasn't sure how to answer that. Even though Zion and I were a couple a week ago, I didn't know where we stood now. "Um, yes ma'am."

"Why do you say it like that honey? Have the two of you broken up?"

"No ma'am, it's just that I haven't heard from him since last week so…"

"Wow! Well, I plan to fix that today. I'd like to invite you to dinner at my house tonight. I've also invited my son, so I'd like it if you came by," she said.

"That's nice of you to invite me to dinner, but I'm afraid I'm going to have to decline…"

"And why is that? Aren't you pregnant with my grandchild?"

Now I was confused. Why would Zion tell her about my pregnancy, but not contact me? I wasn't sure how to respond to Ms. Loretta. I wondered if her son knew that she had invited me to dinner and how he felt about that. I mean, he did ask me to give him some space.

"Yes ma'am."

"So, why won't you join my son and I for dinner?" she asked.

"Well, last time I spoke to Zion he asked me to give him some time."

"Yea, well his time is up. So, will you please join us for dinner?" she asked.

"Okay, sure. I get off at five o'clock, so I'll come when I leave work."

"Great! I'll be waiting for you around 5:30 or six."

"Yes ma'am. See you then."

We ended the call and I went back to work. A couple of hours later, I was sitting in her kitchen when Zion walked in looking all sexy and handsome. My panties immediately moistened as I inhaled his cologne. He didn't look like he was happy to see me. Instead, he looked surprised. I guess his mom hadn't spoken to him about me joining them for dinner. When his mom suggested that I wash my hands before dinner, I figured she was about to give her son the business.

I stayed in the bathroom a couple of extra minutes to give them time to discuss my presence. When I emerged from the bathroom, Zion was sitting at the table and his mom was handing me a plate. As the two of us joined Zion at the table, my knees began to knock due to my nervousness. This was the first time I had been in a room with Zion since I told him the news. I imagined the two of us having a discussion about our future, not sitting here with his mother in the middle as a mediator.

"Y'all so darn quiet. It would seem that two people who just found out they're going to be parents would have more to discuss," Ms. Loretta said. The two of us continued to sit quietly and eat our food. "Well, since you two aren't going to speak to each other, I guess I'll have to do all the talking. Zion, I was informed by Malayka that she hasn't seen you since she told you about her pregnancy. You wanna explain to me why that is?"

Zion casted his gaze over in my direction, making me feel even more uncomfortable than I already was. "You told her that?" he asked me.

"It's the truth."

"You shouldn't have told my mom that!" Zion said angrily.

"Why not? Why didn't you want me to know that you were running away from your responsibilities?" his mom asked.

"I wasn't running away from my responsibilities mom! I just needed some time to think about my next move," he said.

"Your next move? You act like you're playing a chess game or something! This is a baby we're talking about! Your only move should have been to accompany this young lady to the doctor to find out the due date... period!" his mom said.

"You don't understand," Zion said.

"Then help me understand," Ms. Loretta said.

"I'd like some clarity also," I interjected.

"Look Malayka, you and I ain't been dating but for a couple of months..."

"Four..."

"What?" he asked with a questioning look on his face.

"We've been dating for four months. That's two more than a couple."

"Well, it doesn't matter. It's still a short period of time. The last thing I wanted to hear was that you were pregnant," he said.

That kind of threw me for a minute even though I wasn't sure why. I shouldn't have been surprised to hear him say that knowing I probably would've never seen him again if it wasn't for his mom. Tears threatened to fall from my eyes, but I wouldn't let them. As much as it hurt me, if Zion didn't want to be a father to our baby, I'd pull myself together and do it on my own. If my mom did it, I could do it too.

"Zion, if you don't want to be a father to our child, it's cool. Once the baby is born, you can sign over your rights and never hear from me again," I said.

"The hell he will!" his mom said. "I didn't raise my sons to be a deadbeat like their father!" My eyes widened when I heard her say that. I just assumed that his dad had been a part of his life. Hearing his mom say that he had a deadbeat dad like I did really shocked me. If his own father walked out on him, wouldn't he want more for our child? "My son is going to step up and be the father to your child that he never had."

"I didn't say I wasn't going to be in our child's life, Malayka. All I asked for was some time to digest the news."

"Well, was a week long enough or would you like for me to disappear for another week?"

"I'm sorry I left you hanging for the past week. I was just in shock. I always thought when I had my first child I'd be married to the mother. I never wanted to have a baby mama. I wanted a wife, ya know?" he said.

Wait a minute. Was Zion asking me to marry him? Oh my God! I wasn't prepared for this. Don't get me wrong, I'd definitely say yes if he asked because I loved him. Regardless of the fact that we had only been together for a few months, I didn't wanna be just his baby mama either. I took a deep breath and waited for him to get down on one knee and ask me to be his wife.

"I understand," I said as I nodded my head. The tears I had been fighting to hold back finally broke free. These were happy tears though. In a million years, I never thought that the night would end this way.

"But just because we aren't getting married doesn't mean I won't be there for you and the baby," he said. It took me a minute to process what he was saying to me and when I did his words literally crushed my soul. He wasn't asking me to marry him. He had no intentions on asking me to be his wife. He did however; say that he wanted to be there for me and our baby.

"Thank you."

"You don't have to thank me. I watched my mom raise my brother and I by herself. I wouldn't put you through that, so whatever you need, I'm there. Have you been to see the doctor yet?" he asked.

"Yes, I went last week."

"What did he or she say?"

"She said that the baby will come in about five months, 21 weeks to be exact."

"You don't know what it is yet?" Zion asked.

"No, not yet."

"Oh my! I'll be a grandmother by fall," his mom said with a smile. "I can't wait for the holidays this year, especially Thanksgiving because I have so much to be thankful for this year!"

"We both do mom," Zion said as he looked at me with a smile.

I managed to smile back even though it felt as if my insides and heart had been shattered. "Well, thank you so much for inviting me to dinner, Ms. Loretta."

"Oh, are you leaving so soon? You haven't even had a piece of my homemade peach cobbler yet," she said with a look of disappointment as I stood up.

"Oh my! Well, as yummy as that sounds, I'm afraid I have to leave. I've had a long day and I have to wake up early for work tomorrow." That wasn't a total lie... I was somewhat tired, and I did have to work in the morning, but that wasn't my real reason for cutting out so soon. I just couldn't stomach being next to Zion another minute while pretending to be all happy and stuff. I was truly hurt.

She wrapped her arms around me and held me tight. "I'm glad you were able to come. This dinner went even better than I thought it would," she said as she released me.

"It sure did," I lied. This dinner didn't go the way I thought it would, but I sure wouldn't say it went better. I thought that Zion was going to ask me to be his wife, so we could raise our child together. Instead, he just said he'd be there for me. I guess half was better than nothing, right?

"I'll walk you out," Zion said.

"Oh, you don't have to..."

"I know, but I want to," he said as he turned his attention to his mom. "Ma, I'm gonna walk her out and then I'll come back to help clean up the kitchen."

"Okay baby. Bye Malayka, we should do this again sometime," she said.

"Yes ma'am, I'd like that."

I turned and headed for the door with Zion following behind me. I wished he had stayed with his mother. I didn't need anyone to walk me out. I had two good legs and was capable of opening doors by myself. Once outside, he said, "I'm really sorry I didn't contact you sooner."

"It's cool. Everything's all good now, right?"

"Right. When is your next doctor's appointment?" he asked.

"Next month."

"I'd like to be there," he said.

"Sure, I'll send you the details when I get home."

I unlocked the doors to my car and opened the driver's door. I was about to slide into the front seat when Zion gently grabbed my elbow. "Hey, I'm glad we were able to work things out," he said with a smile.

"Yea, me too."

He pulled me into his arms and embraced me. I practically melted in his arms as I inhaled his masculine scent mixed with his cologne. "I still care about you Malayka," he whispered.

"Mmm hmm," I responded. I was way too weak to speak to him.

He pulled away from me for a minute as he stared into my eyes. It had been 12 days since we had sex and I was definitely on the horny side. I pressed my lips to his, not sure how he'd respond. To my surprise, he opened his mouth and hungrily kissed me back. As we sucked on each other's tongues for the next few minutes, my nipples hardened, and I could feel his dick pressed up against me. He pulled away from me and stared into what I knew were my lust filled eyes. Hell yea, they were lust filled because I wanted him. If we weren't outside his mom's house, I would've climbed in the back seat and pulled him in there with me.

"I'll come by once I leave here," he said huskily.

"Mmm hmm," I mumbled with a nod of my head as I slid into the driver's seat of my car. My hand trembled as I pushed the start button to rev up my engine. We waved goodbye to each other as I backed out of the driveway.

I was so excited that Zion was coming over. I hoped that we'd have sex and then things would go back to the way they were before I told him that I was pregnant. I just wanted my man back. I made my way home with my mind solely on finding a way to get me and Zion's relationship back to where it was before.

When I got home, I decided to take a shower since my panties were so wet. As I rubbed my hands over my baby bump, I smiled at the thought of a baby being inside. I couldn't believe that I was having a baby. I still hadn't told my mom yet, but I was going to go over to her place this weekend. I knew she would be excited about being a grandmother, just like Zion's mom.

I turned the water off after about 20 minutes and stepped onto the bathroom rug. I grabbed a towel and dried myself off. Before I had a chance to get dressed, there was a knock on my door. I wrapped the towel around my dampened body and practically ran to the front door. I pulled the door back and immediately fell into his opened arms. The kisses between us were just as hot and feverish as they were when we were at his mom's place not too long ago. He kissed me all the way to the bedroom before dropping my towel to the floor.

He gently pushed me down on the bed and dropped between my legs. "Mmmmm!" I moaned as he sucked on my most treasured goodies. I intertwined my legs around his neck and held him in position as I rotated my hips in circles. I clutched the comforter beneath me as he continued to lick me.

"Oh my God!" I hissed as he continued to feast on me. "Hmmm!"

Finally, after I had two orgasms, he stood up and quickly removed his clothes. He climbed in the bed and drove his dick inside me. I moaned and bit his shoulder as he pummeled inside me. "Oh... my... God!" I moaned in a breathless tone.

"Damn! Pregnant pussy feels good as fuck!"

I had heard that shit, but I wouldn't know. I tightened the muscles of my kitty as he moaned louder. If he thought it was good before, I wanted him to think it was great now. "Oh shit!" he hissed as he kissed me hard on the lips. "Turn that sexy ass around!"

I did as he asked and turned over on my hands and knees. He got behind me and smacked me on the ass before driving his dick inside me. I bit down on the comforter as he plowed into me over and over again. I had forgotten how good our sex life was over the past few days. I had been stressing so much about the pregnancy and Zion's reaction. I just hoped that things between the two of us would just fall right back into place once this little sexcapade was over with.

"Your pussy is so good!"

Our bodies were getting all sweaty as we continued to release our frustrations from the past week. He lifted my ass cheeks up and drove his dick into me like a jackhammer to a sidewalk. I buried my face into a pillow and screamed in pleasure as my insides quivered and my body shook like an earthquake.

As my orgasm rose to the surface, I released the pillow and screamed out loud. "Ohhhh my Gooooodd!" I cried out.

"Don't be calling God to help you!" he said as he continued to hit my G-spot. My whole body was shaking by the time he finally pulled out. He collapsed beside me on the bed as we tried to steady our breathing. By the time my breathing was back to normal, I heard him snoring softly beside me. Dammit! I wanted to know where we would go from here, but with him sleeping all I could do was cuddle up next to him and close my own eyes. I was just as exhausted as he was.

The next morning, my alarm sounded at seven since I had to be at work by eight. I rolled over and Zion was still asleep next to me. As I made a move to get out of bed, he reached for me. He pulled me close to him and asked, "Where are you going?"

"To get ready for work. I gotta be there by eight," I informed him.

"Well, I guess I better make this quick then," he said as he nibbled on my earlobe while rubbing his dick against my ass.

"Babe, I don't have time for this. I don't wanna be stuck in traffic."

"That's why it's called a quickie," he said as he lifted my left leg and drove into me from behind. As he grabbed both of my breasts, he pushed up against me and grinded his hips into my ass from the side. Over and over, in and out he went for I don't know how long. All I knew was by the time we both got ours it was almost 7:45. I knew that I was gonna be late for work, so I grabbed my phone and called my manager before I hopped in the shower.

"Hello," Nina answered.

"Nina, it's Malayka. My alarm just went off so I'm gonna be a little late for work," I said.

"Okay, but please try to get here soon because Esmerelda called to say she wouldn't be in today."

"I'll get there as soon as I can," I said. We ended the call and I turned the water on, so I could take a quick shower. However, I wasn't expecting to be joined by Zion. When he slid the door open and got in behind me, feeling on me and stuff, I was ready to get out. I could not be too late for work, especially since no one else was scheduled to come in until 11.

"Zion please, I have to hurry and get to work," I protested.

"C'mon, I've been deprived of sex for the past week. I need some more," he pleaded.

"You gon' make me lose my job." He kissed my neck and rubbed his dick against my ass. "Aw babe."

"C'mon, you know you want it." He was right too. When he reached for my leg to pick it up, I didn't stop him. When he slipped his dick inside me and pulled me close, I grinded against him. I knew Nina was going to be pissed at me for being later than I intended, but it wasn't my fault. I had even intention on being on time for work this morning.

As he gripped my hips, he continued to slam his pelvis into my backside. Yea, we had definitely missed each other. The feel of his dick inside me had me so delirious that I got my hair wet. I wasn't trying to get my damn weave wet, but I was in a position to lose my mind right now. I didn't know that Zion had missed me this much, but as he pummeled me from behind I realized exactly how much he missed this good good.

By the time we were done, and I had finished getting dressed, it was close to 8:30. I was supposed to be at work a half hour ago. I was so engrossed in what me and Zion had going on in the shower that I hadn't even heard my phone ringing. When I grabbed it off the counter, I checked the screen and saw that Nina had called me seven times. I had three text messages from her also, so I knew she had to be upset.

"I gotta go babe," I said as I hurriedly pecked his lips. "Please lock my door on your way out."

"Yea, I will."

I rushed out the door, even though I could barely move. My body was hurting some from all the activity that Zion and I had participated in. I hurried to my car, hopped in, and headed to work. Thank God there wasn't too much traffic on the way. I was almost to the pharmacy when my phone began to ring. I glanced at the screen and saw that it was Nina calling again. I quickly hit the steering wheel to take the call.

"Hey Nina," I answered.

"Malayka where are you?"

"I'm almost there. I was caught up in some traffic."

"Please hurry."

"I am." I ended the call and continued to drive to my job.

The next couple of days were just like before. I'd get home from work and Zion would be waiting for me in my driveway. I was confident that our relationship was back on track and that he'd be a figment in our baby's life forever. I breathed a sigh of relief because I was happy that I wouldn't be raising our baby as a single parent. I was even more in love with Zion now than I was before I found out I was pregnant. I couldn't wait to go to my next doctor's appointment. I was confident that I'd be far enough along that they'd be able to do an ultrasound.

As Zion and I lied in bed that Friday evening, I relaxed my head on his chest. As I twirled my fingers through his chest hairs, I brought up a conversation I had been dreading for the past few days.

"Zion, I was wondering if you'd do me a favor."

"Wassup?"

"I'm going to my mom's house tomorrow. I wanna tell her about the baby," I said.

"You haven't told your family yet?"

"Well, my sister knows, but I haven't had a chance to tell my mom yet. It's not something I wanted to do over the phone. Since I'm off the weekend, I thought it would be a good idea to go over there and tell her face to face," I explained.

"I agree. I didn't have the opportunity to tell my mom. My brother broke the news to her before I did, so I think it's a good idea for you to tell your mom before she hears it from someone else, especially now that you're starting to show," he said as he ran his hand over my small belly.

"I didn't know your brother told your mom. I thought you told her." I was absolutely shocked that his brother had done that to him. Why tell their mom that I was pregnant? I wasn't having his brother's baby... I was having his baby.

"I didn't have a chance to tell her."

"I'm sorry."

"It's cool. I'm glad she knows. If she didn't know, I probably wouldn't be lying here in bed with you now."

"Really?" I asked.

"I didn't mean it like that... anyway, what is it that you need from me?" he asked.

"I want you to come with me to my mom's house to tell her the news about the baby."

He sat up in bed and ran his hand down his face. "Uh, I don't think I wanna do that."

"Why not?"

"Because that's a moment you and your mom need to share. She don't know me. She probably don't even know that you been messing with me."

"You're right. She doesn't know anything about you, but that doesn't mean you can't come with me."

"Nah, I'm not comfortable with that shit," he said.

"Why not? It's just my mom," I said.

"Your mom who I've never met before. Your mom who didn't know anything about me. Your mom whose gonna know that not only I've been screwing her daughter, but I got her pregnant too. Nah, I ain't comfortable with that."

"Babe..."

"I said no, Malayka... DAMN!!" he said as he hopped out of bed. I watched in shock as he started putting his clothes on.

"Wh-wh-where are you going?" I stuttered.

"Home!" he said as he sat on the bed to put his socks and shoes on.

"You don't have to leave Zion," I said.

"I don't feel like staying here no more. I think it's best if I did leave."

"But why?"

"Because man, you done fucked up my mood! You act like you have no understanding about me or my feelings!" he said. "I said I didn't wanna go because I wasn't comfortable with that shit. How you thought it was gonna go when you trying to force me to do some shit I don't wanna do?"

"I'm sorry! I don't wanna fight with you. We've been getting along so well," I pleaded with tears in my eyes.

"Nah, I'm out! Shit was cool and would still be cool if you had just let it be when I said I wasn't comfortable going with you to your mom's. All you had to do was let it go, but nooooo!" he said as he stood up. He stormed toward the front door with his keys in hand.

"Zion, I'm sorry."

"Yea, whatever!"

"When are you coming back?"

"I'on know. Shit, your guess is as good as mine!" he said as he opened the door and walked out. As the door slammed behind him, I slumped to the floor. This was almost deja vu to the night I told him that I was pregnant. I sat on the floor and cried for two hours before I got up and headed to the shower. I couldn't believe shit had come to this, yet again, just because I wanted him to come with me to tell my mom about the pregnancy.

I guess in a way he was right though. I shouldn't have tried to force him to come with me, especially after he said he'd be uncomfortable. I didn't know what had gotten into me in that moment. I guess I just didn't wanna have to face my mom on my own. But that was my responsibility to tell my mother. I wasn't with his brother when his mom was told. I fucked shit up with Zion all by myself, and now I might have to raise our child alone.

After I cried in the shower, I climbed out and dried off. Then I slipped on a nightgown and climbed into my big king-sized bed by myself. I cuddled up with Zion's pillow and inhaled his scent for the entire night. That was how I fell asleep.

I wished I had listened to Zion that night. Things between us might've turned out differently if I had.

CHAPTER FOUR

Zion

Three months later...

Malayka was so excited about the baby that she wanted a gender reveal party and a baby shower. I talked her out of the gender reveal party because it didn't make sense to have two parties back to back. So, today was the baby shower and everyone knew that we were having a girl. When I found out she was carrying a little girl, I didn't trip about it. I had already told her that I'd be happy with a girl or boy. It wasn't about the gender. As long as our baby was healthy with ten fingers and ten toes, I was straight.

We were having the shower catered, so our family wouldn't have to cook or worry about nothing. We also had a party planner to decorate the venue. That was something that Malayka didn't need to deal with when she was almost eight months pregnant. As I checked out myself in the mirror, I was pleased with the vision that looked back at me.

I chose to wear a pair of white Dockers, a long sleeve button-down Ralph Lauren shirt and a pink Ralph Lauren blazer. I choose my tan colored Stacy Adams dress shoes to complete the ensemble. I looked good in this pink blazer, something I would've never worn a few years ago.

I checked the time on my Fossil watch and headed for the door. The shower was set to begin at two o'clock and it was approaching one. I slid into the sleek seat of my car and headed over to Malayka's house to pick her up. No, we weren't back together. I didn't want to get with her again after what happened that last time we were together. I could do bad by myself without a woman trying to control me and get me to shit she wanted me to do.

She now had a clear understanding of our relationship and that was to be co-parents to our daughter. We had decided to name our little girl Mackenzie. We had a 3D ultrasound last week and used some of the pictures for the baby shower. I thought she had my nose, but we'd just have to wait until she was born to see for sure. I was excited about becoming a father, and even though I wasn't with Malayka anymore, I was going to do everything I could to let my daughter know that I loved her.

I promised my mom, myself and Malayka that I wouldn't be anything like my father and I planned on keeping that promise. I was going to be the best dad I could to my baby girl. She would know that she was loved and wanted. I pulled up to Malayka's house and hopped out the car. I knew she probably needed help with something. I knocked on the door and she opened it almost immediately.

As she stood before me, my dick immediately stood at attention. She looked beautiful. She had on a pink sheath dress the color of my blazer and it hugged her curves in all the right places. As I inhaled her sweet scent, my nose twitched. She smelled like sugar and flowers or some shit like that. I just knew she smelled good as fuck. She had her hair in an updo with some curls hanging. She also had some small pink and white flowers in her hair. If we didn't have to get to this baby shower...

"Boy, close your mouth!" she said as she smiled.

"I'm sorry. You just look so beautiful," I said. She actually took my breath away for a moment.

"Thank you. You cleaned up really nicely yourself. Love the pink jacket," she said.

"It's not a jacket. It's a blazer," I corrected.

"Well, I still love it! Can you help me carry this to the car please?"

She pointed to a huge box with pink baby wrapping paper and a huge pink bow. "What's that?"

"I don't know. It came to the house a couple of days ago, but I wanted to wait until the baby shower to open it."

"Who is it from?" I asked.

"My Aunt Lucinda from California," she smiled.

"You have an aunt that lives in Cali?" I asked as she nodded her head. "I didn't know that."

"There's a lot you don't know, but can you grab the box please. The last thing I want is for us, the parents, to be late for our own baby shower," she said.

"Aight."

As I walked out with the huge and heavy box, I was glad I had traded my sports car in for something more family sized. Instead of the Dodge Challenger that I used to have, I now drove a Ford Explorer. Good thing too because this box would've never fit in the Challenger. Once Malayka had locked her door, I helped her in the truck.

We made pleasant conversation as I drove to the venue. I kept stealing glances at her because my fucking dick was still hard as a rock. I hoped that nigga calmed down some because she and I weren't even on that level anymore. As I pulled into the parking lot, I saw that some of the guests were starting to arrive. I guess we had made it just in time.

I won't go into all the specifics about the baby shower, but I will say that everything was beautiful. We got some really great gifts, ate some fantastic foods, and enjoyed ourselves without any issues. As I loaded most of the gifts in my truck, my brother and Malayka's sister agreed to put some in their vehicles and follow us to Malayka's place.

Once there, as we unloaded the vehicles, I peeped some chemistry going on between Nate and Brianna. I had seen them chatting at the baby shower but didn't think nothing of it. Seeing the two of them together now, I knew there was something going on between them. After we finished putting all the baby things in the nursery, I pulled my brother to the side to have a little convo with him.

"Wassup?" he asked.

"What's going on between you and Malayka's sister?" I asked.

He looked over at her and smiled. She smiled back and tucked a strand of hair behind her ear. I nudged him to get him to pay attention to me. "Nothing much. She's cool people, ya know?"

"Yea? Cool people like how?"

"She just cool people. I mean, I just met the chick earlier, so..."

"So, you like her or you just looking to score? Because if you're looking to score with my baby mama's sister and shit don't work out, that shit is gonna be awkward for everybody," I said.

"Bro calm down! We just met, so don't go jumping to conclusions."

"I'm not jumping to conclusions. I'm just saying."

"Trust me when I say, I'm good. You don't need to give me any advice at this point because we just met. Okay?"

"Aight. Just remember what I said though," I warned.

"Yea, okay. Well, I'm gonna get outta here. Don't do nothing I wouldn't do with yo baby mama if you don't wanna be with her for the long haul. All yo ass gon' do is confuse her," he warned.

"What do you know?"

"I know her sister told me that she's still in love with you and that you hurt her feelings when you walked out on her last time. If you ain't trying to be with her, after we leave, take yo ass home!"

"Yea, aight."

We dapped it up before he walked over to Malayka and her sister to say goodbye. He gave Malayka a hug and said, "Thanks for the invite to the shower. I had fun."

"Thank you for coming Nate," Malayka said.

He turned his attention to Brianna, who was blushing like crazy. What was it with those two? "You aren't gonna give me a hug?" Brianna asked.

"Oh, you want a hug too?" Nate pulled her into his arms as I watched the two of them. For two people who supposedly have nothing going on, it sure looked like something to me.

As she pulled herself from my brother's arms, she turned to her sister and said, "You know what? I'm gonna head out too."

"What? I thought you were going to help me put some of the baby stuff away," Malayka said.

"I'll come by tomorrow to help you. Right now, I'm kinda tired, ya know?" I watched as she winked at Malayka before giving her a hug. She whispered something in her sister's ear that left her mouth hung open. I wondered what the hell she had just said.

She walked over to me and gave me a hug. Then she and my brother walked out of the house leaving me and Malayka standing there looking at each other. "What just happened?" I asked.

"She likes your brother..."

"I KNEW IT!! I KNEW THERE WAS SOMETHING GOING ON BETWEEN THEM!"

"Yea, I kinda saw them flirting earlier too."

"Ain't that some shit?" I asked with a chuckle.

"Yea, it is. Well, thank you for helping me with everything. I appreciated having you there today," she said.

"Where else would I have been? Mackenzie is my baby too Malayka. I'll always be there for you, especially where our daughter is concerned."

"Thanks. The last thing I wanted was to have to raise our baby alone," she said as she rubbed her swollen belly.

"You'll never have to worry about that."

"Well, thanks again."

"Are you putting me out?" I asked.

"Well, I'm kinda tired, sooooo..."

"I thought you wanted to put some of the baby things away."

"I did, but Brianna said she'll come by tomorrow, so I'll just do it then. I'm a bit worn out."

"Yea, I can understand why." I moved over to where she stood and touched her belly. "It won't be long now."

"I know and I can't wait for these next seven weeks to be over with. I just wanna see my feet again," she said with a smile.

"It'll be over soon," I said as I pulled her in for a hug. Once again, inhaling her scent made my dick hard. Before I knew what was happening, we were kissing like two hungry teens. Suddenly, she stopped and pushed herself out of my arms. "What's the matter?"

"We can't keep doing this."

"Doing what?"

"This," she said as she pointed from me to herself.

"What do you mean this?"

"I mean, if we aren't going to be together, we shouldn't keep playing with each other's emotions," she said.

"I'm not playing with your emotions Malayka."

"Oh no?!"

"No. I care about you very much. You're the mother of my first child, so I'll always have feelings for you. It's just that being with you today felt good, ya know? Like when we first got together," I said.

"I know," she said as she avoided eye contact with me. I quickly closed the gap between us and lifted her chin with my forefinger.

As she stared into my eyes, I brought my lips back to hers. I couldn't help how I was feeling in that moment. My dick was hard, and my emotions were all over the damn place. As we kissed our way to the bedroom, we began to shed out of our clothes. I quickly unzipped her dress and slipped it from her shoulders. I had already taken off my blazer and shirt, so I wasted no time dropping my pants and boxers.

As we fell in bed together, it took me all of two seconds to get my meat inside her. I almost busted my damn nut right then and there. I hadn't fucked in three damn months, but I was going to make up for it tonight though. As I gyrated my hips into her pelvis, she cried out in pleasure. Her pregnant pussy felt so good right now. She was biting down on her bottom lip and looking good while doing it. I think my dick grew an extra inch as I brought my lips to hers.

I felt my nut soaring to the surface, so I removed my dick from her juicy folds and buried my head between her thighs. As she tried to push my head from its current position, I wouldn't let her. I continued my oral assault on her until I felt her juices invade my pallet.

"Turn over," I said in a husky voice that matched how I was feeling.

She flipped over and got on her hands and knees as I stared at her jiggly butt. She had put on a few pounds since the pregnancy, but I wasn't complaining because it fit her just right. As I got behind her and prepared to enter her from behind, I smacked her butt. "Put it in baby please!"

"You want this dick?" I asked as I rubbed the head against her soaking wet opening and smacked her ass again.

"Yes, please put it in!" she begged.

"You want this dick?" I asked again.

"Ohhhhh God! Yaaasssss! Stop teasing me please!"

36

I thrust my swollen member hard inside her as she yelped like a puppy. As I gripped her hips, I pummeled her insides hard from the back. She grabbed the pillow and buried her face in it as she screamed. I didn't know why she did that. It wasn't as if her screams would disturb anybody since she lived alone. Her pussy felt like a warm glove wrapped around my thick dick. My shit pulsated as I continued to thrust deep inside her.

"Oh God!" she cried out.

"Your pussy feels so good," I winced.

All of a sudden, my dick exploded inside her. Damn, that was a heavy ass load. I hope I didn't drown my kid in the process. I collapsed beside her on the bed, trying to steady my breathing. She moved close to me and laid beside me.

"I haven't had sex since the last time we did it. I'm worn out," she huffed.

"Me either and me too. All I wanna do is climb in my bed and get to sleep," I said.

She propped herself up on her elbow and stared at me, confusion evident on her pretty face. "You're not staying the night?"

"Nah, if you need some help putting away some of the baby stuff, I'm with it. I'ma help you get that squared away and then I'm out!"

"Why aren't you spending the night with me?" I couldn't help but notice the disappointed look on her face. I didn't mean to disappoint her, but I had to leave.

"Because I don't wanna confuse this relationship."

"I think it's a little late for that."

"How so?" I asked as I sat on the side of the bed.

"Uh, we just had sex! Don't you think that changes things?"

"Changes things how? We both knew where things were before we hopped in the bed together. Why should sex change that?"

"Because I still love you and I wouldn't have slept with you if I didn't think there was a chance for us to get back together."

"You knew we weren't getting back together, Malayka. You were just as horny as I was and that's why we had sex!" I countered.

"I thought we had a chance of getting back together," she said.

"You could've said no," I told her.

"I didn't wanna say no! I want us to be a family, the kind of family we didn't have growing up! Every time we sleep together, I think we're going to work things out!" she said with tears in her eyes.

"I'm sorry if that's what you thought. That's definitely my bad because this relationship is never going to be more than the two of us co-parenting our daughter. Now, you can't say that you don't know where we stand, so next time we decide to have sex..."

"NEXT TIME?! Now that I know you'll never get back with me, there won't be a next time," she said.

"Well, I can understand why you feel that way. Just know that I'm always going to be here for you and our daughter. That means that even if we aren't together, we're still a family. Mackenzie is going to tie us to each other for the rest of our lives," I said.

I wasn't trying to talk her into bed or anything. I just wanted her to know that our child would bring us together forever. She and I would always be family, and that wasn't going to change just because she and I weren't a couple.

"Can you just leave please?" she asked in a soft voice. I knew she was hurting, and I never meant to hurt her. I was just horny and thought she was too. I didn't know she had sex with me because she still wanted to be with me. We hadn't had sex in three months and shit had been going great between us.

I went to all her appointments and was there for her first ultrasound. I was thrilled when we saw our little girl on the monitor for the first time. I guess having sex with her fucked her head up, but that wasn't my intention.

I moved closer to her and tried to hug her. She raised her hand to stop me from getting any closer. With her hand pressed up against my chest, she shook her head. "Just leave," she said.

"Aight." I grabbed my keys and walked out the door. "If you need me to help you with the nursery tomorrow…"

"Maybe some other time, but definitely not tomorrow," she said before closing the door in my face.

Damn! How she gon' get mad at me when she wanted to fuck too? Next time she looking for some good dick, she gon' have to look somewhere else. From here on out, my dick supply for her is cut off.

Who am I kidding? I'm lying. If she wanted me to hit it tomorrow, I'd be right back between her legs. It wasn't my fault though. She had some good pussy from the start, and now that her pussy was pregnant. Lawd, I couldn't resist. But for the sake of our working to parent our baby together, I would do my best to refrain from giving her anymore of this good wood.

I hopped in my ride and headed home.

CHAPTER FIVE

Brianna

"**O**h shit! Yea, right there! Right there!" I hollered as Nate fucked me hard from the back. How did I end up in this situation and position with a man I just met earlier today? Well, I don't have an answer for that. All I knew was that when I met him, I felt drawn to him immediately. The fact that he was related to my sister's baby daddy didn't deter those feelings at all. I didn't intend to end up in the bed with Nate. When he said he was leaving from my sister's earlier, I decided to leave also. I figured the two of us would grab a bite to eat and call it a night.

However, once we got to talking, it turned out that we weren't even hungry. I invited him to my place for a nightcap and one thing led to another. I was shocked at how quickly my clothes came off for this man. He was a stranger to me, yet that didn't seem to matter to my purring kitty. As I held my pussy open for him to go deeper, my head started spinning. I didn't know why we hadn't met sooner.

Here I was, single and ready to mingle, and my sister had been keeping this fine ass man from me for the past eight months. "Mmmmm!" I moaned as I arched my back for him to hit my G-spot.

"Aw shit! I'm about to cum!" Nate groaned as he gripped my butt cheeks. I felt his dick throbbing inside me as my own orgasm reached the surface. He shoved his dick in one last time before his body began to shake.

He hopped out of bed once he had pulled his dick out and headed to the bathroom. I knew he was about to flush the used condom and wash up. I mean, ain't that how shit went? He returned about five minutes later and fell beside me on the bed. He stretched out his arm and I relaxed my head on it as we tried to return our breathing to its normal state.

"Girl, you trying to get me hooked?"

"No, believe me when I say that I never intended for this to happen," I said.

"You had me at hello," he said.

"What does that mean?"

"It means that from the moment you said hello to me, I was putty in your hands."

"Putty huh?"

"Yep, I ain't scared to say how I feel," he admitted.

That was nice to hear. A man who wasn't afraid to tell a woman how he felt was hard to find these days. "That's a good thing. Most guys these days are scared to let a woman know how they really feel."

"Not Nathan. I ain't scared of shit!" he said as he straddled me.

"What are you doing?" I asked.

"I'm about to share my feelings with you," he said as he rubbed the head of his dick against my kitty.

"Wait! No glove, no love."

"C'mon, I'll pull out."

"You better."

He shoved his meaty pole into me and I wrapped my legs around his waist. He drove into me over and over again. By the time we were done for the evening, it was mid-morning and I was exhausted.

The next morning, I woke up feeling so good, I slipped out of bed and went to the kitchen. Since Nate was nice enough to share his feelings with me, I felt he deserved a good meal. I pulled out the eggs, bacon, biscuits from the freezer, grits and ham. I was going to make this man a meal fit for a king. I didn't know where things were going with us, but I was willing to ride it out. If he knew that I could cook in the kitchen and the bedroom, maybe we had a shot at making a go of it.

I mean, I was single, and he was single, so as far as I was concerned, we were good. When I was done cooking, I placed the food in two plates and carried them and some orange juice on a tray to the bedroom. He was stirring when I walked into the bedroom.

"Nate," I called out to him.

"Hmmm," he mumbled.

"I made breakfast."

He turned to look at me. As he wiped his eyes, he looked from me to the tray of food. "You cooked for me?"

"Well, you did work overtime last night," I said as I blushed.

"You got that right!"

He sat up in bed and pulled the cover over his lap. I sat next to him and placed the tray between us. He leaned over and kissed me, morning breath and all. It shocked me that I actually didn't mind him kissing me before he brushed his teeth. We sat and ate breakfast while we continued to talk and get to know each other better. There was one question I wanted the answer to but was afraid to ask. I just didn't want to ruin our great morning.

"So, where do we go from here?" Almost as if he had read my mind, he asked the question that had been replaying itself over and over again in my mind.

"I was wondering the exact same thing," I said.

"Well, I've been single for a while now and you're the first chick that I clicked with this fast in a long time. My brother didn't think it was a good idea for us to get involved..."

"What? How does he know?"

"He doesn't, but I guess I was staring a little too hard at you yesterday, so he kinda put two and two together. He gave me this lil warning before we left, but as you can see, I didn't listen."

"Why not?"

"Well, for one, my brother got his own issues with your sister, so he ain't in no position to be handing out advice to me. And two, my personal business is just that... my personal business. What I do and see is no one else's business but my own," he said.

"So, are you going to tell him about us?"

"Sure, when the time is right. I ain't finna run my mouth to him now because I wanna see where this goes. So, what do you wanna do?"

"I'd also like to see where this goes. It took me this long to find you, so I'm not even thinking about letting you go," I said.

He leaned over and stuck his tongue in my mouth. "You ain't gotta let me go," he said.

I wasn't one to believe in fairy tales and shit, but I did believe that this thing between Nate and I was real. I'd be a fool if I passed up the opportunity to see how far this relationship could go. We had great chemistry and that was a great factor in any relationship.

As we removed the food tray off the bed, we buried ourselves in beneath the covers for the rest of the day. Nate left around nine o'clock Sunday night because he had to work in the morning. He would've stayed if it wasn't for work. His apartment was closer to his job than mine was. If he had stayed over at my house, it would've taken him over an hour to get to work. I didn't want him to be on the road that long just, so we could keep playing house.

He promised to call the next day. I was a little bummed because we wouldn't be able to see each other until the following weekend. I wanted to call my sister as soon as Nate left, but knowing that his brother didn't want to see us together made me keep that to myself. I went to bed feeling good as hell. Nate texted me when he got home.

Nate: I really had a good time

Me: Me too. I can't wait to see you next weekend

Nate: Ikr. I'm about to hop in the shower and hit the sack. U wore me out

Me: U wore me out 2

Nate: Good night sweetie

Me: Good night boo

I put my phone on the nightstand and buried myself in the covers, inhaling Nate's scent from the pillow he slept on last night. When I say I went to sleep as soon as my head hit the pillow, that's exactly how it happened. I was totally exhausted.

CHAPTER SIX

Malayka
Seven weeks later...

"**P**ush Malayka! You got this!" Zion coached as I bore down and pushed the way I was told to do. This had to be one of the hardest and most tiring experiences of my life. I didn't know how some women could have so many kids back to back. Once I pushed Mackenzie out of me, I wouldn't be looking to have any more kids for a long time.

It felt like I was trying to push out a watermelon out of a sweet pea. I had decided to not get the epidural because I had heard so many stories about women who still had pain in their lower back because of it. I didn't want to risk that happening to me, so I decided to go with a natural labor. The pain was excruciating and a couple of times, I wanted to change my mind, but I didn't. I had read that the natural labor experience was less harmful to me and my baby.

One thing I was happy about though was that Zion kept his word about being here. Even though we hadn't been sleeping together and hadn't gotten back together, he was still there for me when I needed him. He and his brother put the nursery furniture together while my sister and I put the baby clothes in the closet and drawers. The four of us worked well as a team, but I now realized that Zion and I weren't meant to be together.

My sister and Nate however were a different story. I was shocked to find out that they had been seeing each other since the baby shower. They seemed to be really into each other and I was happy for them. I just remembered a time when Nate and I had the same kind of bond. Of course, that was before I found out I was pregnant. I hoped my sister and Nate took their time before they decided to start a family. Zion and Nate were brothers so that could mean birds of a feather flocked together and not in a good way either.

"Come on sissy, you can do it!" Brianna said as she held my hand.

43

Once again, I lifted my back up from the bed and began to push. My mom, sister along with Zion and his mom were all in the room with me. I couldn't believe the four of them were here during one of my most vulnerable moments. This was definitely a joyous occasion but having them be able to see my coochie spread open like that was a little embarrassing.

I leaned back against the bed as the doctor said, "Okay Malayka, on the next contraction I'm going to need one more big push from you. Ready?"

I nodded my head even though I was exhausted. Even though I had only been pushing for a couple of hours, I was still very tired. As I continued to push while they counted, I soon felt a huge relief from my bottom. A couple of seconds later, I heard my baby's cries echoing through the hospital room. I finally leaned back against the bed and breathed a sigh of relief. I was a mother now. I was going to be totally responsible for this perfect little human that Zion and I created.

As I watched Zion clip the umbilical cord, he looked every bit the proud papa. The doctor placed the baby on my belly as I stared into her beautiful little eyes. Tears flowed from my eyes as my mom and sister embraced me, telling me how proud they were of me. The baby was taken from her comfortable spot and brought over to the incubator with the light. Zion rushed over and stood in awe of his little girl.

He looked over at me with a huge smile. "She weighs eight pounds and six ounces," he said.

"Damn sis! That's a big baby!" Brianna said.

"Who you tellin'?" I remarked with a smile.

"My baby did great! You were a champ, just like yo mama!" my mom said as she kissed me on the forehead.

"Thanks mom," I said. Zion's mom stood next to him with tears in her eyes. She looked over at me and smiled with a wink. Ms. Loretta had been a huge help the past few months. I appreciated everything she had done to get Zion on track. "Thank you all for being here."

"Are you kidding? Where else would we be?" my mom asked.

"I'm gonna go let Nate know that the baby here. We'll come back in after you get cleaned up," Brianna said happily. She stopped by the incubator and took a quick picture of the baby before walking out the door.

The doctor finished patching me up and stood up. "I have another delivery, but I'll be back to see you again soon," she said. "You have a beautiful baby girl. Congratulations to you both!!"

"Thank you, Doctor Celeste," I said as she waved and walked out.

The nurse walked over to me and handed the baby to me. She had advised me to pull my gown down and give the baby a chance to bond with me, skin to skin.

As I held my baby girl in my arms, I marveled in her sweet baby scent. She had smooth jet black hair and chubby cheeks.

"Have you decided if you're going to breast or bottle feed your baby?" the nurse asked.

"I'm going to use the bottle," I stated.

"Are you sure? I'm only asking because we always advise new mothers to breastfeed. Breast milk is actually better for your baby because it contains antibodies that will help her fight off viruses and bacteria. Breastfeeding also lowers your baby's risk of having asthma or allergies. Not only that, but babies who drink only breast milk for the first six months, without any formula, have fewer ear infections, respiratory illnesses, and diarrhea. It's totally up to you of course," she said with a smile.

I looked over at Zion to see what he had to say. I had thought about bottle feeding Mackenzie because eventually I'd have to go back to work and that would mean I'd have to pump milk to leave for the sitter. "That's okay. I'll use the bottle, thank you."

"Okay, I'll go get some premade bottles for you to use while you're in the hospital. I'll be right back," she said as she left the room.

"She's so beautiful," Zion said as he rubbed her small back.

"Yes, she is baby. Y'all did good," Ms. Loretta said.

"Yea, she's so beautiful," my mom gushed.

Having Zion, his family and my family here made today even more special. I absolutely loved my daughter. Today had been the best day of my life... literally.

The past couple of months, Zion had been staying with me in my house to help me with the baby. I truly appreciated him for that because I didn't know how I'd do it without him. At least with him here, we both took turns waking up with Mackenzie, so we wouldn't be totally exhausted. Zion was the best dad Mackenzie could've asked for.

Thank God Zion's job gave him paternity leave, so he didn't lose out on any money while he was helping me the past eight weeks. My mom, sister and his mom were also great at lending a hand. Zion and I had worked out a child support and visitation agreement amongst ourselves. I was glad that we were able to do that because that meant we didn't need to involve anyone else.

I had a few friends who had children for men who didn't want to take care of their kids. Because of that, they had to seek help from the child support division just to get the fathers to accept financial responsibilities. That was sad that they had to do take those steps. What would make a man not feel the need to take care of his own child? I hoped I never had to find out the answer to that question. I prayed that Zion would continue to do right by Mackenzie.

◆ ◆ ◆

Fast forward four years later...

Things between Zion and I had been going great. Mackenzie was a happy, well-rounded little girl. She was very smart and well-mannered. I didn't know being a parent would make me this happy. I knew that Zion was a good guy and he cared a lot about our daughter. He was the epitome of a great father, everything his father and mine weren't. We shared joint custody of our daughter. I had her during the week and Zion had her every other weekend. Sometimes, he'd pick her up from daycare and take her over to his mom's until I got off. All in all, he was a great dad.

I started noticing little changes in Zion's behavior about a month ago. It wasn't anything major, but it was enough of a change for me to ask him about it. I mean, he used to pick Mackenzie up from daycare at least twice a week. The past month, he only picked her up three times. He even missed one of his weekends with her because he had gone out of town. That wasn't like him at all. He had always been so responsible and dependable when it came to our daughter. Lately, the Zion I had been seeing wasn't the same one who came home with me from the hospital. One evening, he came by to drop off Mackenzie, he was in such a rush to leave, that he was forgetting to hug and kiss our daughter goodbye. I knew I had to say something to him because if I didn't, I'd regret it.

"Mackenzie why don't you go put your things in your room? Mommy needs to talk to daddy for a minute," I said.

"Can this wait? I really have somewhere I need to be," Zion said with an anxious attitude.

"No, it can't wait."

"Bye daddy," Mackenzie said as she hugged her dad.

"Bye baby," Zion said.

Mackenzie raced out of the room, dragging her Trolls backpack behind her.

"What's this about?"

"Where are you off to in such a rush? I mean, lately it seems like you're always in a hurry. Not only that, but you've been shirking on your responsibilities to our child," I said.

"Shirking on my responsibilities? What are you talking about Malayka?"

"You've been a great dad the past four years, but lately, it seems as if you've changed."

"I haven't changed. I've just been busy," he said with an attitude.

"Too busy for your own child?"

"How am I too busy for my child when I just had her this past weekend?"

"You missed the previous weekend."

"Look Malayka, obviously you're upset and taking out your frustrations on me," he said.

"I'm upset because you haven't been..."

"Haven't been what Malayka? I missed one weekend... one fuckin' weekend!! Damn!"

"Don't take that tone with me! Our daughter is right in the next room," I hissed through clenched teeth. "All I wanted to know was why you've changed so much."

"That's not your business," he said as he took a defensive stance.

"I'm just asking a question that concerns our daughter. It seems as if the past month, WHEN you show up, you've just been throwing Mackenzie in the house."

"Throwing her in the house? I do NOT throw my child in the house!"

"You know what I mean. You were about to leave a few minutes ago without telling me how your weekend with her was or anything. You weren't even going to kiss her goodbye!"

"That's a lie! I wouldn't have left and not given her a hug."

"So, how was your weekend? What'd you guys do?" I asked.

"Our weekend was great, and we had fun! Now, if you're finished with this damn inquisition, I'm gonna go," he said.

"Well damn! I didn't realize asking about your weekend with our daughter was an inquisition!" I said as I crossed my arms over my chest.

"You know what? I gotta go."

With that, he turned on his heels and rushed out of the house. I watched him hop in the truck that I didn't know was running and that was when I saw her. That explained why he was in such a rush to leave. He had some other chick waiting for him in the truck. What kind of shit was that? How could he disrespect me like that and bring his bitch to my house?

My heart broke when I saw that woman in the truck with Zion. I knew that he had other females in his life. I certainly didn't expect him to be celibate for those years we had been apart. But to have a bitch come between him and his daughter wasn't something I ever expected. I pulled out my phone and called him.

"What?" he answered.

"Was that why you were so quick to run outta here... because you had some chick in your truck waiting on you?" I was fuming and pissed all the way off.

"Malayka, who is in my truck should be no concern of yours. You don't run me."

"Who's around my daughter concerns me a hundred percent of the time. But was that why you were so quick to run up outta here?"

"Look, I ain't trying to argue with you. Mackenzie is home, so go spend time with her and get off my damn line!"

He didn't give me a chance to respond. He hung the phone up in my face after he said what he needed to say. I walked to my baby's room and sat down on her bed. She was sitting in the middle of the bed with tears in her eyes.

"What's wrong baby?" I asked.

"Why were you fussing with daddy?" she asked with all the innocence of a four-year old.

"I wasn't fussing with daddy. We were just talking. I'm sorry if mommy got a little loud." I tried to soothe and comfort her, but inside, I was still pissed. It wasn't that I had an issue with Zion having a girl in his life. Hell, he had them before that one and I was sure he'd have them after her. I just didn't like how he was tossing his fatherly obligations to the side for some random.

"How was your weekend with daddy?" I asked.

"Good. We went to the zoo and I got to pet the animals," she said.

"That's great baby. Did you have a good time?"

"Yes, and Krystal is nice too."

"Krystal? Whose Krystal?"

"Daddy's friend."

"So, daddy's friend stayed at his house with y'all?"

"Yea, she slept in daddy's room," she said. "Is she going to be my new mommy?"

You see? That was the shit I didn't like. Why have some random bitch around our daughter and have her questioning me like that? I didn't know what the deal was between him and this chick, but you could best believe I was going to find out.

"No one could ever be your mommy because I'm your only mommy, sweetie. You're my baby girl," I said as I pulled her close to me. "Now, let's go take your bath and get you ready for bed." I walked over to her dresser and pulled out a pair of clean panties and a nightgown.

We walked hand in hand to the bathroom as she talked about the animals she saw at the zoo. I ran the bath water and added the bubble bath to it. When the water was at the desired level, I began to remove Mackenzie's clothes to put her in the tub. As I removed her shirt, I saw a bruise right above her left elbow. When I touched the spot on her arm, it caused her to wince a little bit.

"Baby, what happened to your arm?"

"What?" she asked with a worrisome look on her face.

"You have a little bruise on your arm. What happened to you?"

"Oh, I bumped it," she said as she stepped into the tub quickly. She lowered herself in the bubbles and began to play with her toys.

"When did that happen?" I asked.

She just shrugged her shoulders and kept playing in the bubbles. I decided not to dwell on it. As long as my daughter is okay, I wouldn't let it bother me too much. I finished giving my baby a bath then dressed her and put her to bed. Before she fell asleep, I read her a bedtime story which was something I had been doing since she was six months old. I absolutely adored Mackenzie and I thought that Zion did too. If he knew what was good for him, he'd better get his act together.

CHAPTER SEVEN

Zion

A couple of months ago, I met this chick named Krystal. I met her through my brother Nate. He knew her from his job. She seemed like a cool chick and she was mad sexy, so of course, I asked her out. I didn't expect us to hit it off so quickly, but we did. It didn't take us long to decide to try an exclusive relationship. I introduced her to Mackenzie a month ago. This past weekend was the second time they had seen each other and spent time together.

I couldn't believe Malayka was trying to give me grief about Krystal. I didn't know what she was worried about though because Krystal wasn't trying to take her place or anything like that. I didn't even tell Mackenzie that Krystal was my girlfriend. I introduced her as my friend. So much Malayka was nosey. All she had to do was go on about her business and tend to our daughter. Instead, she was trying to find a reason to pick an argument.

"That was your baby's mama?" Krystal asked.

"Yep. I knew it would only be a matter of time before she started trippin'," I said.

"What's she trippin' about though?"

"It's nothing, babe. Let's just ignore it."

"Okay, if you say it's nothing, then it's nothing."

"Right."

We headed back to my place and got busy until we fell asleep. I liked that Krystal let me handle my own damn business. She didn't put up any arguments or anything like that. If I said let it go, she did just that... she let it go. Malayka was the total opposite. She never let shit go because she seemed to like starting arguments. I knew that Malayka was still in love with me. I knew that because for the past four years, she had been trying to get back with me. Not only that, but she hadn't gotten a man since me. I didn't know what she was waiting on because I moved on.

◆ ◆ ◆

I hated that I had to cancel my weekend with Mackenzie. Krystal had gotten us some tickets to go to the football game, and I couldn't pass that up. I hated having to call Malayka about it even more. I knew she was going to blow a gasket, but what the hell did she want me to do? Even though I knew I had responsibilities to my daughter, I had to have some kind of life for myself too. I still saw Mackenzie during the week, so it wasn't like I was just blowing her off completely.

"Hey Zion, are you on your way to pick up Mackenzie?" she asked.

"No, we're actually going out of state for the Texan game on Sunday. I was calling to ask if I could get Mackenzie the following weekend," I said.

"What?! You're canceling on her again?"

"I'm not canceling, I'm postponing til the following weekend," I reasoned.

"No, you're canceling because this is your weekend. How could you do that to her again?"

"Damn it Malayka! Why can't you just gimme next weekend without all the drama?"

"Because this is YOUR weekend!"

"Well, I won't be here..."

"Why couldn't you go to the next Texan game, huh?"

"Because Krystal got us tickets for this one..."

"Krystal? Who the fuck is Krystal?"

"Krystal is my girlfriend."

"Wooow! You just got a new bitch in your life and now she's more important than your daughter!" she said. I could tell that she was angry with me, but for her to say that shit to me was uncalled for. I had been there faithfully every other weekend for the past four years. These past few weeks were the first time I had ever asked her to do something like this.

Yea, I missed a weekend, but so what? Some fathers missed every weekend, including mine. My father was never there for my brother and I but I wasn't like that. I was there for my daughter since the day she was born. I'm always going to be there for her, no matter what Malayka thought of me right now.

"Look, no one and I repeat, no one is going to come between me and my daughter. You're always reading too much into shit and trying to play me. I'm a good fuckin' dad, no matter what you say or think right now. I'm gonna encourage you to get yourself a life because you definitely need one."

"The fuck! Who the hell are you to tell me some shit like that?"

"Well, I'm not trying to tell you what to do, but you keep coming at me with some bullshit, eventually I'ma throw that shit back at you. I'm just asking if I could get the baby next weekend instead of this one. It ain't nothing that requires help from a rocket scientist. It's either yes or no," I said.

I was sick and tired of Malayka's shit. She needed to get her a man to fuck her good, so she could stop acting stupid with herself. This shit right here was one of the main reasons she didn't need to get pregnant. I had no regrets concerning Mackenzie at all. She was the most beautiful, awesome and precious little girl. I just wished her mom wasn't acting the way that she was. All I wanted was to be able to co-parent with her to the best of my abilities. What the hell was so hard about that?

"Fine! But I'm not gonna keep covering for you like that. If you keep putting your child off for some bitch..."

"Aye, there's no need for the disrespect!" I warned.

I mean, she hadn't even met Krystal yet, so I didn't know why she was calling her out her name that way. There was no need for that and it was going to have to stop.

"Well, what kind of woman would be okay with a man disregarding his child? Ain't nobody but a bitch that would put up with some shit like that!" she said angrily into the phone.

"She's not making me disregard my child! I'm not even doing that shit! I'm going to get her next weekend. You know what? I'm done talking. You're being completely irrational about this shit, so I'm done!" With that, I ended the damn call. She had a lot of fucking nerve trying to tell me who I could and couldn't see. I didn't need her approval on any woman I chose to date, as long as she was cool with Mackenzie that was all that mattered to me. Krystal and Mackenzie got along great!

Malayka called my phone about four times after that, but I hit the ignore button on all her damn calls. There was no way I was going to talk to her right now. This shit was only going to get worse if we spoke again. I never thought that we'd be arguing about a woman I was dating. I never saw the shit coming. What was the problem with switching up my weekend anyway? It wasn't as if I said I wasn't going to come see Mackenzie at all. I just said I would see her next weekend instead because we got tickets to the game.

A couple of minutes later, my phone dinged which signaled a voicemail message. I dialed the number and listened to the message that Malayka had left on my phone.

"Zion, up until now, you've been an excellent father to our daughter. I won't allow your random bitches to swoop down and fuck up our family. No matter who comes in our lives, Mackenzie is always supposed to come first. If you can't put our daughter before your bitches, then we're going to have to discuss the arrangements of our agreement. I'd hate to have to take this to the courts to get help when we had been doing so well before. I sure hope your little getaway is worth everything you're risking to lose. You need to do some self-reflecting and realize that the bitch you're seeing isn't good for you or this family. Don't forget to pick Mackenzie up from daycare Tuesday and Thursday next week."

"Damn it!" I said as I banged my hands on the steering wheel. Did it really have to come to this? Malayka was being completely unreasonable right now. Talking about taking me to court and shit. What the hell did we need court for? I paid child support and took my daughter every other weekend. Not only that, but I picked her up from daycare two or three days a week. We had a good thing going so I couldn't understand why she'd be willing to fuck that up just to prove a stupid point. Wasn't Mackenzie the most important aspect of this whole thing?

I think Malayka was allowing her jealousy to make decisions for her. That shouldn't be the issue at all. Her feelings had no business getting involved in what was best for Mackenzie. Why couldn't I have a woman and keep the great relationship I had with my baby mama?

CHAPTER EIGHT

Malayka

I was livid when I hung the phone up with Zion. How could he do this to Mackenzie? She was looking forward to her weekend with her dad and he had just blown her off. As upset as I was though, I didn't have time to fume about it. My sister was coming by to pick me up because we had some errands to run. She and Nate were getting married in two weeks, so we had a lot of ripping and running to do. My mom would have to pick Mackenzie up from the daycare today since Zion canceled and I knew that Brianna and I wouldn't be done by the time it was time for her to leave for the day.

Brianna pulled up in my driveway a short time later and blew the horn. I grabbed my purse and keys, locked the door, and headed to her car. I slid into the front seat as Brianna leaned in for a hug. "What's the matter with you?" she asked.

"Girl, I'm pissed. Zion called to cancel his weekend with Mackenzie..."

"WHAT?! WHY?!" I was glad to see that she was just as upset as I was. Now, I knew I wasn't making a big deal out of nothing as Zion had made it seem.

"He called and said his new bitch had tickets to the NFL game Sunday and they were going to go. So, he asked if he could get Mackenzie next week instead," I finished.

"Oh, well I can see why he'd want to reschedule his weekend. I'd love to get tickets to the Texans game!" she said with a smile.

"Really Brianna? Whose side are you on?"

"I'm on Mackenzie's side and I don't see anything unreasonable about his request. It's not as if he's blowing the baby off or anything. He just wants to reschedule until next weekend."

"You don't get it, do you?" I asked as I smirked at her.

"Apparently, I don't. I'm not understanding why you're so upset about this," she said.

"First, he went out of town and only saw her one weekend that month. Now, he's going out of town again..."

"But he's rescheduling. He's just swapping this weekend for next weekend. That means, he'll have her two weekends in a row," she reasoned.

"No, he won't. You're getting married weekend after next, so Mackenzie needs to be with me, so I can get her ready."

"Well, that works out perfectly then. You needed to swap weekends with him anyway."

I hated when my sister didn't take my side. I mean, did she always have to be so political about it? Why couldn't she just see how I felt and take my side sometimes? I didn't want her to think rational or nothing like that. Just listen to me and say she understood and that I was right.

"Brianna, why can't you ever just take my side?" I asked the question that had been playing in my head for the past five minutes.

"What do you mean? I'm your sister, so I'm always on your side."

"No, you're not. You're sitting here taking Zion's side over mine. It's not fair because you're MY sister, not his!"

"Are you serious right now? You're really upset because I'm not?"

"I'm upset because you're not listening to my point of view."

"I am listening to your point of view, Malayka. It's just that you're trying to pick an argument with this man for something so simple. He wanted to have next weekend instead of this one. Big deal! You needed to swap the following weekend anyway, so it worked in your favor. Why are you trying to find reasons to battle when there is none?" she asked as she turned her gaze to me for a second. "Are you jealous that Zion is seeing someone else?"

"What? That's absurd! Why would I be jealous of some bitch I ain't never met?"

"She seems like a nice enough woman though."

"You met her?"

"Well yea. Nate and I went to dinner with them a couple of weeks ago," she admitted.

"And you're just telling me this now?"

"Because I didn't want you to get all in your feelings like you're doing now. You haven't even met her yet and you're calling her a bitch. I just think you're jealous because Zion found someone else and you were hoping to get back with him."

"Fuck Zion! I didn't wanna get back with him!"

"Yes, you did and that's why you're acting out like a five-year old. Zion has moved on. He's been moved on, so you should do the same. Sitting around twiddling your thumbs while waiting for him to come back to you is ridiculous! Move on Malayka!" she advised.

"What makes you think I haven't moved on?" I asked.

"Okay, have you? I mean, how many partners have you had since you and Zion broke up? How many men have you let scratch that kitty cat since your baby daddy?" she asked as she stared at me. "I'm waiting."

I couldn't even answer her because the truth was I hadn't let no one else in my life since Zion. I didn't want another man to hurt my feelings the way that he had. Besides, I didn't need a man right now. My daughter was all I needed.

"Just what I thought... the answer is nobody! You need to start going out more. You need to get you some dick!"

"Stop it!"

"I'm serious. Dick is the key to everything! Good dick that is. Get you a man with some good dick and you won't have shit to worry about anymore. The shit that Zion does won't even bother you because you'll be too dickmatized to care," she said.

"Whatever girl," I said.

"Well, how about me and Nate hook you up with someone?"

"No thanks!"

"Why not? Are you going to keep pining over Zion forever? He has no interest in getting back together with you."

"We have a child together. Eventually..."

"Eventually, you'll realize that Zion doesn't want a relationship with you anymore, except for co-parenting Mackenzie. Then what?" she asked.

"Can we talk about something else?"

"Okay but think about what I said."

How could I not think about what she said? I knew she was just being honest, but damn. That shit really hurt my feelings. In two weeks, I was going to have to walk down the aisle with Zion and pretend that I didn't want it to be us getting married. How the hell was I going to do that when I still loved him? Ugh! I just wished I could get rid of these damn feelings I had for my baby daddy!

Two weeks later...

Today was my sister's wedding day to Zion's brother. I had been trying to psych myself up to walk down the aisle with Zion for the past week. The wedding rehearsal last night was definitely one to remember. He brought his bitch with him and pissed me off once again. Why did he have to bring her? She wasn't a part of the wedding. She had no business being there. If she wanted to attend the wedding, she should've just waited until tomorrow like everybody else who wasn't involved.

As I was standing there talking to some of the bridesmaids, Mackenzie screamed out for her daddy and took off running in his direction. I turned my head in the direction and saw him holding hands with some chick with a bad weave.

"Is that Zion's new girlfriend?" Stacey asked.

"I guess so," I responded.

"She's cute," Brenda said.

"I love her hair," Val remarked.

"I know right. It looks expensive," Lacie remarked.

I wished they would shut the hell up, but since I couldn't count on them doing that, I left and went over to where my mom and aunts were sitting. The rehearsal was due to start in ten minutes. All of a sudden, my stomach felt like it was tied up in knots. I could smell Zion's cologne as he walked closer to where I was seated.

My mom leaned over and whispered in my ear, "I need you to act your age and not your shoe size."

I cut my eyes in her direction with my lips pursed together in a thin line. "What?"

"I know how you feel about Zion, but he's moved on and you need to do the same. Don't you go making a scene at your sister's rehearsal or wedding. This is her time and you need to put everything else on the back burner," she warned.

"Hello mom, Ms. Sophia, Aunt Fancy, Malayka," he said as he waved to everyone while holding Mackenzie in his big strong arms.

Seeing how happy Mackenzie was to see her daddy and hearing the words my mom had just spoken to me had me feeling some kind of way. Zion hugged his mom and kissed her on the cheek. Everyone exchanged their hello's as I sat there quietly. My mom always said if I didn't have something nice to say, don't say anything at all. So, I didn't have shit to say.

"Malayka, can I speak to you for a minute?" He placed Mackenzie on the floor and she went to sit next to her grandmothers. "Mackenzie, mommy and daddy will be right back."

"Okay daddy," Mackenzie said happily.

I didn't say anything. I just stood up and started walking until I was a few feet away from everyone else. It wasn't until I turned around that I saw the chick with him.

"Uh, I thought you asked to speak to me. I didn't realize she was going to be a part of this!" I said as I looked the girl up and down with my arms over my chest.

"I just thought I should introduce you to Krystal."

"And who told you that now would be a good time to do that shit?"

"Nobody. I mean, we're in the same place right now, so I didn't want things to be awkward between the three of us. She's going to be at the wedding tomorrow, so..."

"Soooooooo..." I stood there with a quizzical look on my face. This wasn't how I planned to spend my evening, looking at my ex and his new bitch wasn't my idea of a good time.

"So, Krystal this is Malayka, Mackenzie's mother. Malayka this is my girl, Krystal," Zion said with a smile.

"It's nice to meet you," the bitch said. She stuck her hand out to shake mine. I knew I should've been the bigger person and shook her hand, but I wasn't. How could I be the bigger person when this bitch had my man in her clutches.

I just stared at her hand and rolled my eyes. "Malayka, really?" Zion asked.

"How did you expect me to react, Zion? Why would you bring her here? It's nothing but family here. She's not family!" I said as I eyed the chick.

"Look Makayla..."

"Ma-lay-ka! Are you really serious about this chick who can't even pronounce the mother of your child's name correctly?" I asked Zion.

"Are you really trying to do this here?" Zion asked, anger written all over his face.

"As a matter of fact, I'm not. This is my sister and your brother's special time. I won't let you get me upset enough to ruin it for them," I said as I tossed my hair over my shoulders and walked away.

I walked over to my sister and asked, "Shouldn't we be starting the rehearsal right now? I mean, we do have a bachelorette party to get to this evening, ya know?"

"Yes, Yolanda is about to line everybody up. Speaking of bachelorette party, I kinda invited Krystal..."

"YOU DID WHAT?!" I yelled. It seemed as if everybody in the hotel turned to face me.

"Ssshhhh!" my sister said as she smiled at everyone. She pulled me toward the exit and continued. "Now, I'm gonna need you to put on your big girl panties and grow the hell up Malayka! She's dating my husband's brother. How would it have looked if I didn't invite?"

"I'm your sister! Your loyalty should lie with me! Who cares how it would've looked to other people?" I hissed.

"Malayka please..."

"I can't believe you did that to me," I said and rushed toward the restroom. I pushed through the door and went into the bathroom stall. I punched the door and walls of the stall a couple of times before I calmed down. I walked out and toward the mirrors. As I stared at myself in the mirror, I dried my tears.

I took a deep breath, smoothed my off white fitted dress, and walked out. I knew that I looked good, so I wasn't going to waste any more time focusing on Zion and his new bitch. Fuck him and her. I sashayed my ass into the hotel ballroom and took my place next to Zion.

"At some point..."

I lifted up my hand to stop him from speaking. "This is our siblings' wedding, so can it not be at this point. Thank you," I said as I stared ahead.

Nate and his mom were the first ones to walk down the aisle. Then it was the bridesmaids with the groomsmen. When it was our turn to walk, I made my way down the aisle with Zion as if nothing was wrong. I fake smiled my way all the way to the altar. I went left, and Zion went right. I looked to the doorway to see Mackenzie and the little ring bearer walking down the aisle together. They were so cute.

Finally, my mom walked my sister down the aisle and she met Nate at the altar. As we went through the motions of the rehearsal, I smiled at my sister. I couldn't believe she was getting married, but I was truly happy for her. I had hoped that Zion would've come to his senses and asked me to marry him. I mean, we deserved to be a real family. After all, we did have a daughter together.

But I realized now that I needed to move the hell on.

Once the rehearsal was over, we headed to the rehearsal dinner. From there, the women went their way and the men went theirs. I hated that my sister had invited that woman to her dinner, but what could I do about it? I wasn't going to let it worry me one bit. I decided to do as my sister suggested and put my big girl panties on. I was going to drink my ass off and enjoy myself, no matter what.

CHAPTER NINE

Zion

I wasn't sure what Malayka's problem was, but it wasn't my concern. She was acting so fucking childish right now. This was my brother and her sister's wedding, but she was acting like a spoiled five-year old. How dare she behave that way when I was trying to do the right thing. I wasn't trying to introduce Krystal to cause any problems. But Malayka was Mackenzie's mother and I thought it would ease the tension in the room if a proper introduction was done. I should've known Malayka was going to act the fool with herself. Shit, she didn't even wanna shake Krystal's hand.

I knew she was trying to make this weekend all about her, but I wasn't going to give her the satisfaction. I wasn't going to let her know how badly she got under my skin with her attitude. Instead, I was going to plaster a huge smile on my face and get through this for my brother's sake.

As the two of us walked down the aisle for the rehearsal, it took everything in me to not go off on her. For the sake of the wedding, I decided to hold off and tell her about herself when I saw her next week. We made it through the rehearsal okay, then it was time to head over to the club for my brother's bachelor party. I promised Brianna that I wouldn't keep her out too late and that he'd be at the wedding on time tomorrow.

They had their own little bachelorette party going on tonight. I was glad that Brianna had invited Krystal to the party and prayed that she and Malayka found a way to get along. My mom was watching Mackenzie tonight because Ms. Sophia decided to attend the bachelorette party with the women.

"I want you to have fun tonight and not let Malayka get under your skin," I said to Krystal as we said our goodbyes outside the restaurant where the rehearsal dinner had taken place.

"I promise to not give her a second thought. I think she wants you back," Krystal said.

"Well, it's way too late for any of that shit! I'm completely wrapped up in you," I said as I gave her a kiss.

"You better stop before we end up back home."

"You're right!" We laughed as I gave her another kiss. "I'll see you when you get home."

"Okay. Don't do nothing I wouldn't do," she warned.

"You don't have anything to worry about."

"Okay, I love you," she said.

"Love you too," I said as I kissed her again.

Krystal and I weren't living together, but she did spend the night a lot. She was going to come over once she left the bachelorette party. That way she and I could ride together to the wedding. I was excited for my brother and his bride, even if she was Malayka's sister. The two of them were like night and day. Brianna was more reasonable, but Malayka was just a straight fool.

We climbed on the party bus and headed to the strip club. I was going to have to monitor my brother's drinking, so he'd be able to make the two o'clock ceremony tomorrow afternoon. I realized what a task that was going to be once we walked in the club. It was ass shaking and titties bouncing everywhere. Bottles were popping like they cost two dollars each instead of $50.

"Lord, help me get me and my brother home in one piece," I prayed as I downed a shot.

The next day...

I opened my eyes to find Krystal's fine ass lying next to me butt ass naked. What's a man to do? I pulled my boxers off and mounted that big ass before stuffing my burrito between her tight pussy. She yelped from the surprise intrusion, but quickly arched her back as I got to work. She was so wet and juicy that before long, I could see her cream on my dick. That made me wanna go harder as I buried my dick deep inside her moist folds.

"Aw shit!" she cried as she pulled me into her.

"That feels good?" I asked.

"Fuckin' right! Fuck me harder!" she demanded.

I gripped her hips and plowed into her while her thick backside jiggled against my stomach. Her pussy felt so damn good. She tightened her vaginal muscles around my dick which caused my knees to squake. I wondered why women did that shit, not that I minded. It's just that when she did that, I never wanted to get out of the pussy. I continued to hit her G-spot as she moaned louder.

"Come ride this dick," I said huskily.

"Ssshhhiiidd! You ain't said shit but a word," she said as I removed my pipe from her insides and laid on my back.

She took my dick in her hand, which was sticky with her juices, and brought it to her lips. I watched as my pole disappeared in her mouth as she deep throated me. Oh God that shit felt good. My fucking toes were curling as she continued to suck my dick while stroking it with her hand. This was one thing Malayka ain't ever done. Even though I pleased her orally, she never once sucked my dick. She said that shit was nasty. Can you believe that?

I mean, of course it's nasty, but it's a part of sex. Sometimes, a dude liked having some good ol' sloppy, nasty sex, right? I didn't hold that shit against Malayka though. I mean, if she didn't wanna suck my dick, it was her prerogative. I wasn't going to force her to do it because it wasn't that serious. Maybe one day she'd meet a guy and finally realize that oral sex should be pleasurable to both people involved and not just one.

After sucking my dick for a few more minutes, Krystal mounted my pole and slid down. She slid so far down that her ass cheeks were in my lap. As she grinded into me, I tried to touch her heart with my shaft. She bit down on her bottom lip as she moaned. Seeing her facial expressions as I plowed upward made me think of some of those pretty girls on Pornhub. They always wanted to look pretty for the cameras as they took that dick.

Krystal was a very pretty girl. She stood at 5'10, which I loved since I was 6'3. That meant I didn't have to strain my back too much when we kissed. She had luscious lips, smoky grey eyes, a beautifully shaped chin, high cheekbones and her body was shaped like a glass Coke bottle. Just POW! POW! POW! She was what The Commodores referred to as a *Brick House* back in the day. She loved to wear weave in her hair and I didn't trip about that.

Sometimes, she wore it short. Sometimes, she wore it long. Sometimes, she wore braids. Of course, she hadn't done all those different styles for me yet, but I followed her page on Instagram, so I saw all her different looks there. She was really beautiful and the fact that she had over 200,000 followers let me know that she was the shit.

As she continued to ride me, I pulled her face to mine and stuffed my tongue inside her hot mouth. I flipped her over in one swift motion onto her back and climbed on top. I lifted her legs on my shoulders and pummeled her as she cried out in pleasure.

"Oh shit! I'm gonna cum!" she whined.

"Go ahead and cum on this dick, baby!" I begged.

I watched as her body shook beneath me like she was feeling the aftermath of an earthquake. Well, I guess she was. I felt the pressures of my dick about to burst, so I pulled out and released on her stomach. Even though we went raw sometimes, I took every precaution not to have another child right now. It wasn't that I didn't want more kids. It's just that I wasn't ready for another one at this time. Who knew what would happen further down the road between me and Krystal? But for right now, I was enjoying things between us the way that they were.

When Malayka and I got together, we were having so much fun. Being with her was a blast and the fact that we were falling in love with one another made it even better. But then, she had to go and get pregnant. Hell, the relationship was still brand new, so her pregnancy at that time wasn't something I wanted to deal with. She should've done us both a favor and gone to the women's clinic and handled her business. Not that I had any regrets about Mackenzie now that she was here. She was the light of my fucking life and such a beautiful little girl.

I just wished that Malayka had given me some options. Now that I was 27, I'd probably handle things differently if Krystal told me that she was pregnant. I just didn't think that now was a good time for us to have a kid, especially since our relationship was so new. I just wanted us to take our time and explore things about each other before complicating things with a pregnancy.

I planted a kiss on her lips before sliding out of bed to go get a wet wipe to clean off her stomach. I returned and wiped the sperm off her belly and returned to the bathroom to flush it down the toilet.

"Babe, what time is it?" I asked.

"10:30," she said.

"Why don't we hop in the shower and then we can go have breakfast or something? I gotta meet up with Nate at the hotel in a couple of hours," I explained.

"Okay, sounds good to me."

She slipped out of bed and walked her fine ass over to where I was standing. My dick was jumping like a kid with a jump rope. She smiled at the sight as she kissed me while stroking it.

"Damn girl, you gon' make me fuck you again and be late," I said.

She smiled as she bit down on my bottom lip. "Then we better get started."

She walked over to the shower and turned the water on as I watched her every move. I might be sprung like my brother said, but y'all have to understand how I got that way. Krystal was the total opposite of my baby's mother. She was tall, fine, and confident. When Krystal walked in a room, people's eyes immediately averted her way because of the confident strides she took. That woman had me completely blown away.

She stepped in the shower and asked, "Aren't you coming?"

"Ssshhiidd! Try and stop me," I said as I made my way to the shower.

I climbed in behind her and my dick immediately sprang to life once again. I squeezed her perfectly round melons as I kissed the nape of her neck. My dick was knocking on her back door, but I turned her around and lifted her up. I held her tight as she placed my dick inside her. She wrapped her arms around my neck as I slid her up and down my meaty shaft. As I penetrated her love tunnel, she moaned in my ear.

"I love you," she crooned.

"Aw fuck! I love you too," I said as I pushed my dick deep inside her. I gripped her ass cheeks and plowed into her with full force. She continued to moan in my ear as I hit her G-spot with rapid fervor.

I didn't know how long it took for me to release, but I pulled out and sprayed the semen down the drain. She kissed me hard on the lips, her tongue deep inside my mouth as I still held her in my arms. Finally, I placed her feet back on the cool tile floor and we began to clean each other off. Once we rinsed ourselves, I turned the water off and we stepped out. We each grabbed one of the huge towels and dried ourselves off before heading to the bedroom to get ready for brunch.

The time now was 11:20, so we'd have to bring our clothes we were going to wear and head to the hotel after we were done eating. Once we got dressed and loaded all our stuff in the truck, I called my brother.

"Where you at man?" he asked.

"Leaving the house."

"Good. So, you're on your way here?"

"Uh, not exactly. Me and Krystal was about to get something to eat first. Then we were gonna head over there."

"Nigga, it's my wedding day! You're my best man! I need you here to keep my ass in line like ASAP!" he said.

"Wassup? You got cold feet?"

"Not really, but my nerves bad as fuck. I mean, I ain't ever had no wedding before. I ain't ever been married to no chick before. I feel like I'm gonna throw up one minute, then the next I'm fine. Dude you gotta get over here!"

My brother sounded like he was panicking big time. I'm sure that feeling to throw up was from the liquor he consumed last night. I had no doubt that he was nervous because I knew if I was in that situation, I'd be nervous too.

"Bro, I'm gonna be there soon, but I haven't eaten yet. I gotta put something on my stomach before I come over there," I said.

"Fuck all that! I'ma order you a turkey club sandwich and some fries from room service. It'll be here when you get here," he said.

I looked over at Krystal and she nodded for me to get over there. "Make that two orders and we're on the way," I said as I held her hand and kissed it.

"Aight, bet. Now, get yo ass over here! Shit, I'M GETTING MARRIED!!" he said with a nervous laugh.

"We're on our way bro. Hold tight."

I ended the call and looked over at Krystal. "I'm sorry bae. I wasn't trying to take you over there so soon."

"It's cool. I'll wait in the restaurant at the hotel. I can grab a bite to eat there while you spend time with your brother," she said.

"No, you don't have to do that. The second sandwich I had him order is for you. When you're done eating, you can head over to Brianna's room."

"Uh, you're kidding, right? I am not going to go to that room knowing your baby mama is in there waiting to start some shit with me," she said. "No, thank you."

"That's okay babe. I'm sure your brother hasn't eaten yet, so he can eat the second sandwich. I'm gonna chill in the restaurant until 1:30 and then I'll head to the ballroom."

"Are you sure? I mean, it's only noon," I asked. I was a bit concerned about her spending so much time in the restaurant. "I got an idea. Why don't I rent a room and you can go there when you're done eating? That way, you can get dressed in the privacy of your own room and we can spend the night there because I know I won't feel like driving back home."

"I like that idea," she said with a smile.

"I don't know why I didn't plan that shit sooner. I guess my nerves are just as bad as my brother's huh?"

"I guess so. Just remember that he's the groom."

"I already know," I said with a smirk.

We pulled into the hotel's parking lot a short time later. I parked my truck, and we got out and retrieved our things out. We walked over to the receptionist's counter and the girl plastered a huge smile on her face.

"Hello, how may I help you?"

"I was wondering if I could get a room," I said.

"King or double beds?" she asked.

"King."

"Do you want a suite or a regular room?"

"Just a regular room. It's only for tonight," I said.

"May I have your ID please?"

I reached in my back pocket and pulled out my wallet. I handed her my driver's license as she entered the information into the computer. "Okay, your total is $190.88," the girl said.

Damn! I didn't know why I was shocked by the price. After all, this was The Embassy Hotel and shit around here reeked high prices. I pulled out my Discover card and handed it to her. She slid the card and handed the ID and credit card back to me.

"Will you be needing two keys?"

"Yes."

"Okay, I just need you to sign here and I'll get your keys ready," the girl said.

I signed the receipt and put my cards in my wallet. The girl returned a short time later and handed me the keys. "You're on the second floor, room 218. When you get off the elevator, you'll make a right and follow the hall. Thank you and I hope you enjoy your stay at The Embassy," she said with a smile.

We made our way to the elevator and hit the arrow that would take us up. When the elevator came to a halt, we climbed on. As the doors were closing, we heard someone say, "Hold the elevator please!"

I stuck my hand in between the doors to keep it from closing. When Malayka hopped in the car, I wished I had let the door close. "Thank you," she said until she saw it was us on the elevator. "Ugh!"

I didn't even bother to say anything as we waited for the elevator to come to a stop. When it stopped at the second floor, Krystal and I grabbed our things and exited. Once we got in the room, she turned to me and asked, "Was your baby mama always that immature? I mean, did it turn you on when she whined and pouted worse than her child?"

"She wasn't always like that babe," I said.

"You can't get me to believe that. I wish you didn't have to deal with her."

"I know. I wish I didn't have to deal with her either. Unfortunately, we have a child together, so she's going to be a part of my life forever."

"Forever? Just the thought of dealing with her for that long would have me running for cover," she said.

"Really? So, does that mean you wouldn't marry me if I asked you?" I said as I wrapped my arms around her waist.

"No, it doesn't mean that and don't tease me. We've only been dating a couple of months..."

"So... my brother and his bride were only dating four months when he decided to pop the question. Of course, I talked him out of it. I told him to give it more time since they hadn't known each other that long."

"And here they are, four years later, getting married."

"Yea, he asked her two years ago, but you know how you women want that fairytale wedding and shit," I said with a wink.

"Yep. Anyway, you'd better get up there to your brother's room before he starts calling you again," she said.

"I know. Are you sure you're gonna be okay?"

"Babe, c'mon, I'm not a little kid. I can take care of myself for a couple of hours. Go handle your business," she said.

"Aight. I love you."

"Love you too," she said.

I grabbed my stuff and headed upstairs to my brother's room on the fourth floor.

CHAPTER TEN

Krystal

I gotta admit that when Zion first told me he had a child, I wasn't too pleased with the idea of dating a man with a kid. I had heard some awful stories about the lengths the baby mama would go through just to keep the baby daddy in her clutches. The last thing I wanted was any baby mama's drama. But then I met little Mackenzie she changed my mind. I thought maybe dating a guy with a little girl wouldn't be that bad. She was beautiful and sweet, all the things I'd love if I had a child.

Then I met the baby mama from hell. That bitch had an attitude and didn't care who knew about it. I mean, if I was co-parenting with a dude I would hope that I'd respect his right to be with who the hell he wanted to be with. Just because a woman had a child for a man didn't make that man hers to keep forever. Zion and his baby mama had broken up long before I came into the picture, so I didn't understand what her issue with me was. Maybe she had an issue with him, but that had nothing to do with me.

I felt that she was behaving like her child should've been. I mean, surely her four-year old didn't have more maturity than she did. The scene she made at the rehearsal last night didn't make any sense and was uncalled for. I stuck my hand out to shake hers and she just left me hanging and made herself look like a damn fool. I guess she had some fantasy that she and Zion would be together since they had a child together, but he didn't feel that way. Had he felt that way about her, he never would've gotten with me.

The bachelorette party was another thing. I'm sure I was invited by Brianna because she and I were dating brothers. Last night, I tried to enjoy myself because I hadn't been out in a while. However, having that bitch around the whole night watching me made it almost impossible for me to be myself. I didn't even drink as much as I would've if she hadn't been there. I hated that Malayka had to be there.

I really wished that she wasn't a part of Zion's life, and from what he admitted a little while ago, he wished the same thing. The fact that they had a child together made it impossible to get that bitch out of his life any time soon. I didn't know how much longer I was going to have to deal with her blatant disrespect. I know you were probably thinking that I should walk away from Zion since we hadn't been dating that long, but I loved him.

I didn't know what it was about him, but I fell head over heels with him almost instantly. I had been dating Zion for a month before I met his daughter. She was a sweet little girl and she seemed to like me. However, with a mother like Malayka, I was sure she'd turn against me sooner or later. As much as I cared about Zion, I didn't know if our relationship would last long with that bitchy baby mama in his ear.

After I freshened up my face, I left the room and headed to the restaurant downstairs. I decided to get something light to eat because the wedding was in less than two hours. I knew there was going to be some good food at the reception, so I didn't want to get too full eating here. I was seated at a table and when the server came to take my order, I ordered a house salad with a glass of red wine. I sat at the table until my food came. When I was done eating, I checked my watch to see what time it was. It was almost 1:30, so I paid my tab and went back to my room. I needed to shower and change so I could make it to the ballroom before the ceremony began.

Once I was dressed, I looked at my reflection in the mirror. My burgundy dress clung to my curves and I loved the way it looked on me. I had my hair down and I wore some silver slingbacks. I looked good as hell.

I made my way downstairs and found a seat near the aisle. I wanted to be able to see Zion when he walked down the aisle and I wanted him to see me too. Right at two o'clock, the music started to play. I guess some black people really did know how to be on time for something. I turned my attention toward the entrance and watched as the bridesmaids and groomsmen began their trek down the aisle.

My attention was solely focused on Zion, but he hadn't come through the doors yet. Nate looked handsome and his mother looked every bit the proud mama. Finally, Zion and that witch began walking down the aisle. He winked at me when he spotted me while that bitch rolled her big ass eyes. Once they were at the altar, I turned my attention to Mackenzie and the little boy. They looked so cute as they walked together.

The door closed as we were asked to stand for the bride. Everyone stood up and turned their attention to the door again as it opened to reveal Brianna and her mom. She looked so beautiful in an off the shoulder style mermaid dress. It was fitted at the top and flared at the bottom with lots of ruffles. The top had lace and beading on the bodice and it fit her beautifully. She wore a beaded headpiece around her head that matched the beading on her gown. She had a beautiful lace veil that also matched the lace on her dress. She looked like a beautiful princess.

Luckily for me, I knew some of the guests who attended the wedding. This lady named Monica whispered to me, "Isn't she beautiful?"

"Yes, she really is."

As Brianna and her mom walked down the aisle, the music played. Brianna had tears in her eyes as she walked to Nate, and he had tears in his also. As he dabbed at his tears with the back of his hand, my eyes teared up. Once the two of them made it to the altar, Brianna hugged her mom and she hugged Nate also.

Brianna's mom took her seat in the first row and Mackenzie went to sit with her. As I watched the exchange between Nate and Brianna, I couldn't help but look at Zion and his baby mama. I caught her gazing at him with love in her eyes. Ugh! Watching her stare at him pissed me off.

I realized in that moment that I was going to have to find a way to keep her from Zion and if that meant keeping him from his daughter, then so be it. From here on out, I was going to do everything in my power to keep him from Mackenzie and that bitch ass baby mama of hers.

CHAPTER ELEVEN

Malayka
Four months later...

My sister and Nate had a beautiful wedding. They had been married for a few months now and were happier than when they first started dating. I didn't think they could be happier than that, but I guess the fact that they were expecting their first baby had a lot to do with that. I was thrilled that Mackenzie was going to have a little cousin to play with in a few months. I was happy for the two of them and I couldn't wait until their baby was born.

Zion had promised that things between us wouldn't be so strained, but they were worse now than ever. I knew it was because he had that new bitch in his life and I was tired of it. Every time my baby went to visit with her dad now, I worried that his bitch would try and turn my baby against me. I figured instead of waiting for that to happen, I'd beat her to the punch. I sat with Mackenzie every day and spoke to her about Krystal. I mean, she wasn't anyone important to me. She didn't even need to be in my daughter's life anyway. It wasn't as if she was a stepmom and Mackenzie had to bond with her. She was actually a bitch who had taken her daddy from us and I told her so.

"Mackenzie honey, you're going to your daddy's house tomorrow. Do you remember what mommy said about daddy's girlfriend, Krystal?" I asked.

She nodded her head slowly.

"What did mommy say about her?"

"That she was an evil witch from faraway who had come to take my daddy from me."

"That's right honey. I know that daddy wants you to like Krystal, but that's because he's under her spell. Don't fall under her evil spell baby because if you do, we won't be able to free your daddy from the spell."

"How can we break the spell mommy?" she asked in a worrisome tone.

71

"We just have to treat her like the evil witch she is and eventually, she'll go away. Then, you, me, and daddy and can be a happy family again," I said.

"But won't daddy be mad at me?"

"Why would he be mad at you honey? You're saving him from the witch," I coached.

"Last time I called Krystal a witch, daddy said he'd punish me," she said sadly.

"Your daddy adores you baby. He isn't going to punish you at all."

I coached my daughter until she went to bed that night, and again the next morning on my way to drop her to the daycare. One way or another, I was going to get that evil bitch out of her daddy's life. Krystal didn't belong with Zion; I did.

When Sunday rolled around, I waited for Zion to drop Mackenzie off at my house. I had called him earlier and asked that he drop her here instead of my mother's house. He didn't sound too happy though, but that was okay. I knew it was probably because Mackenzie had turned on his bitch and he was sulking about that. I didn't care. Mackenzie was my daughter, so there was no way I was going to let that evil bitch take her from me.

At six o'clock, I heard Zion's truck pull into the driveway. I rushed to the window to see if his pit bull was in the passenger's seat and was rejoicing when I didn't see her. Maybe my plan to get rid of her worked. I mean, if I were involved with a man who had a baby with someone else, I wouldn't wanna be with him if his little girl didn't like me. What good would it do her to be in Zion's life if the daughter didn't like her ass?

Zion walked up to the front door and I opened it. "Hey baby," I said as I greeted my little one with a hug.

"Hey mommy, I missed you!"

"I missed you too pumpkin. Did you have a good weekend with your daddy?"

She looked sadly at Zion and then at me. "What happened?" I asked as if I didn't already know.

"Mackenzie, come give daddy a hug and kiss goodbye," Zion said as he squatted to her level. "Remember what daddy said, okay? I love you very much and no matter what, I'll always be your daddy and I'll always, always love you."

"I love you too daddy," she said as she wrapped her small arms around his neck.

He kissed her on the cheek and said, "Go put your backpack away, so daddy could talk to mommy."

"Are you guys gonna fight?" Mackenzie asked sadly.

"Oh no, honey!" I assured her as I dropped down to her level. "Daddy and mommy are just gonna have a conversation. I promise that we won't yell or argue."

"Okay." She walked slowly down the hallway and closed the door to her room.

"I'm gonna go put the television on for her and get her settled. There's some beer in the fridge if you'd like one. I also have some Patron in there too, just in case you need to relax because you look super stressed."

"Just go get Mackenzie settled and get your ass back out here!"

"Uh, well excuse me!" I said as I rolled my eyes. I nervously walked to Mackenzie's bedroom and turned her TV on. I put it on one of her favorite cartoons, kissed her forehead, and headed back out to the front room.

When I walked into the living room, Zion was pacing back and forth. "You're gonna burn a hole in my carpet if you keep doing that," I said with a smile as a way to break the tension.

"What have I ever done to you to make you hate me so much?" he asked.

"Hate you? What do you mean hate you? Zion I still love you," I said as I tried to touch his cheek. He grabbed my wrist and threw my hand back at me.

"I don't know how many times I have to tell you that whatever we had before is fuckin' over!" he hissed through clenched teeth. "Even if I end up alone without a woman by my side, which is exactly what you're aiming for, I won't ever get back with you!"

"What is this about?" I asked as I crossed my arms over my chest.

"All that bullshit you've been telling Mackenzie about Krystal has got to stop."

"I'm so confused..."

"Quit lying Malayka!" he said. I could see how angry he was, but I didn't care. I had no intentions on letting that woman fill my shoes as my daughter's mother. "I know that you've been telling Mackenzie that Krystal is a witch, an evil witch. You told her that Krystal was a witch that came to take her daddy from her? How could you stoop so low?"

"I don't know what you're talking..."

All of a sudden, Zion ran up on me and got in my face. "You're a fuckin' liar! Where else would a four-year old get some shit like that from if it didn't come from you?"

Damn! He really was mad and blaming me for his mistakes. What the hell had gotten into Zion these past few months? I was asking the question, but I already knew the answer. That voodoo queen had some kind of spell on him. I was going to break him out of it if it was the last thing that I did.

"I only told Mackenzie that Krystal wasn't right for you," I lied.

"And who are you to say that shit? Who the fuck are you to know who is or isn't right for me? This is my fuckin' life and I will make that determination, NOT YOU!"

"Damn! You must really care about that bitch. Otherwise, you wouldn't be acting so stupid!" I taunted him.

"I do love her, and you know what else?"

"What?"

"I'm gonna marry her too."

"WHAT?!" I asked as I tried to keep my tone down. I didn't want to upset Mackenzie when we promised her that we wouldn't fight.

"You can't marry her! You've only known her for a few months," I said. Inside my whole body was quivering. My nerves had me on pins and needles. How could Zion even think about marrying that bitch? I had known him for five fucking years and he didn't even consider marrying me, even though I was the mother of his child. What the hell made that bitch so special that he would pop the question to her and not me?

"It doesn't matter how long I've been knowing her. I'm still gonna ask her to marry me and you can't do shit about it. So, if I were you, I'd just stop with all the bullshit because once we're married, then what are you gonna do?"

"Zion please, you can't marry her! She's not good enough for you," I pleaded.

"And who is? You? You think you're good enough for me with all the scheming and shit you've been doing. You've been using our daughter to do your dirty work and I don't appreciate that shit!"

"I haven't been using my child to do anything!"

"Yes, you have and it's gonna stop! No amount of bullshit you're feeding Mackenzie is going to make me break up with Krystal to take you back. We are over and the sooner you realize that, the better off you will be because then you can move on. I'm tired of telling you that I don't love you. Shit, to be honest, I don't know if I've ever loved you. It's just that you were saying it, so I started saying it..."

"What are you saying? Are you really saying that you never loved me and that you lied to me when you said that you did?" I asked. If he was trying to hurt my feelings, he definitely was doing that. My heart felt like it was breaking into a million tiny pieces. The one thing that had kept me going all these years was the fact that he had loved me. Now he was standing there telling me he didn't think he ever loved me. How could he not love the mother of his only child? I couldn't even keep the tears from flowing because I was truly hurt.

"So, you never loved me?" I asked through cloudy eyes.

"No, I don't think I ever did. I'll tell you why. I have feelings for Krystal that I ain't ever had for another woman, including you. When I'm away from her, I think about her all the time, like now. She's waiting for me at home and I can't wait to get back to her…"

"At home? She's living with you now?"

"Yes. She moved in with me two months ago. That's why I keep telling you to move on because I have. You need to stop this shit and stop trying to turn our daughter against her. Eventually, I'm going to marry her, and I want Mackenzie to get along with her stepmother. So, all this other bullshit has to stop, Malayka," he said.

I clutched my chest because I felt the burn of his words for the first time. Not only did he say he loved that bitch, but she moved in with him and he planned to marry her. Where did I go wrong? What did I do that was so bad that he couldn't love me that way? I thought I had done a good thing by becoming the mother of his firstborn child, but now I see that didn't matter at all.

"Can you leave please?" I asked.

"Not until we come to an understanding. Are you going to stop with the bullshit?"

"I want you to get out of my fuckin' house before I call the police!"

"Damn! There you go with that bullshit again," he said.

I walked over to the door and opened it. "Don't make me have to tell you again," I said.

He shook his head and walked toward the door. "If you don't stop telling my daughter that shit you've been telling her, I'm going to get a lawyer. I'm sure he can draw up something to keep you from spewing out your venom on our daughter."

"GET OUT!! GET OUT OF MY HOUSE!!" I screamed.

He finally walked out, and I slammed the door and locked it. I couldn't believe this had happened. I dried my tears, straightened my posture, and made my way to Mackenzie's room. I opened the door and peeked in on her and she was sound asleep. I turned the television off and put the nightlight on. I left a crack in the door and went to my bedroom. I turned the water on and hopped in the shower. That was the only place I could let go of my true feelings without waking my child up.

I slid down the shower wall and cried my eyes out. I literally felt the pain in my heart as I cried like a kid at Christmas who didn't get anything. I couldn't believe my whole world had been turned upside down in a matter of minutes. What was I going to do now? I had done everything I could to get him back and it had only pushed him further into her arms. Life just wasn't fair.

When it was Mackenzie's turn to go visit her dad again, I didn't tell her anything. What could I tell her? The damage had already been done. It didn't seem as if anything I was doing was ever going to change Zion's mind or bring him back to me. I decided to go to church that Sunday and put it all out on the table. I wanted to share my pain with God and hopefully, he'd lead me in the right direction. By the time I left church, I felt a little better.

I had prayed, cried, and gave it to God. I wasn't going to let Zion, or his witch cause me anymore pain. As I waited for him to drop off Mackenzie, I wondered how I'd react when I saw him today.

When his truck pulled up, I stepped outside and waited for Mackenzie to get out of the truck. Imagine my surprise when she stepped out and I saw a huge knot on her forehead. I immediately raced over to her without any shoes on my feet at all. "What in the hell happened to her forehead?" I shrieked.

"She was playing, and she fell," Zion said as he shrugged his shoulders.

"She fell? What the fuck was she on... the Empire State Building?" Of course, I was exaggerating, but I didn't care. My baby had a huge lump on her forehead and that shit scared me.

"Really Malayka?" Zion asked.

"Did you have something to do with this?" I asked the bitch in the passenger's seat as I glared at her. She just looked at me with a wicked grin on her face. "Let me find out that you had anything to do with this and I will whoop yo monkey ass!"

"Bitch please, ain't nobody scared of you! Your baby fell," Krystal said.

"I bet you had something to do with it!"

"Malayka, just take Mackenzie in the house please. You're making a scene in front of those nosey ass neighbors of yours," he said through clenched teeth.

"I don't give a fuck! LOOK AT MY BABY'S FACE! LOOK AT IT!" I screamed. "DID YOU AT LEAST TAKE HER TO THE DOCTOR TO MAKE SURE SHE DOESN'T HAVE A CONCUSSION?"

"No, because that's not necessary. We put ice on it and gave her Tylenol for the headache. She'll be fine in a couple of days," Zion said.

"What kind of father are you? Why aren't you more concerned about your daughter's condition?" I asked.

"I'm gonna go before I say something that I'll regret." He leaned down and scooped up Malayka in his arms. "I'll see you on Tuesday sweetie. Daddy loves you."

"I love you too Daddy. Bye Krystal!" Mackenzie said as she waved to that bitch.

I took her from Zion and took off speed walking toward my house. I couldn't believe this shit. Lately, it seemed like if it wasn't one thing it was another.

I sat with Mackenzie in my lap and kissed her cheek. "How did this happen, baby?" I asked. I just knew that her dad hadn't told the truth.

"I just fell, mommy," she said.

"But how did you fall to make such a knot like that?"

"I just fell."

That right there made me really suspicious. How the hell did she just fall but not have any other details? If she truly fell, she'd be able to tell me how she fell, what she hit, something. But she couldn't tell me anything.

I'd find out though. Right now, I had to tend to my baby girl, but you could mark my words when I said that this shit wasn't over. I knew that bitch had done something to my daughter and I'd find out one way or the other. Zion might have rose-colored glasses on, but I sure didn't. I could see everything as clear as day and that bitch had something to do with my baby girl getting hurt.

Once I got Mackenzie to bed, I went outside and called Zion. I needed to know why he didn't call me as soon as that shit happened. It made me think that if they could've got the swelling down, they wouldn't have told me.

"What now Malayka?" he answered.

"Why didn't you call me when Mackenzie hurt herself? Why would you keep something so important from me? I'm her mother!"

"I know you're her mother. I could never forget that you're her mother," he said.

"What the hell is that supposed to mean?"

"Malayka look, I'm sorry that we didn't tell you about it when it happened. Krystal thought..."

"KRYSTAL?! KRYSTAL?! WHAT THE HELL DOES SHE HAVE TO DO WITH THIS ZION?! MACKENZIE IS OUR DAUGHTER... YOURS AND MINE! NOT HERS! JUST BECAUSE YOU CLAIM TO LOVE HER, THAT DOESN'T MAKE HER A PART OF THIS FAMILY! IF SOMETHING HAPPENS TO OUR DAUGHTER WHEN SHE'S IN YOUR CUSTODY, I HAVE A RIGHT TO KNOW ABOUT IT!"

I was pissed to the tenth power that he had even mentioned that bitch to me. She had nothing to do with any decisions involving our child. She was just a body that was sleeping with the man who should've been mine.

"You're right, and I'm sorry. I didn't mean to not tell you. I just didn't want you to worry. We had it handled and did everything we could to make sure that the swelling didn't get too bad."

"What's all this we shit Zion? The only we that has anything to say concerning our daughter is you and I. That woman has nothing to do with Mackenzie. You shouldn't have let her talk you out of telling me because she's my baby. I should've known right away!" I said as tears streamed down my cheeks.

"I know Malayka, and there's nothing else I can say except sorry."

"Zion, our baby has a knot on her forehead! How can you not be concerned about that? I just need you to tell me how that happened. Weren't you watching her?" I asked. I was fuming mad, but I was trying to keep my anger at bay until I found out what really happened. I just wanted him to tell me that his bitch had something to do with Mackenzie's condition.

"She was jumping on her bed and I guess she fell and hit the floor," he said.

"You guess that's what happened? So, I'm guessing that you weren't in the room," I said.

"No, she was in the room with Krystal."

"So how do you know that she fell on the floor?"

"What? I'm not understanding your question," he said.

"What if she was pushed off the bed?"

"Okay, now you're trippin'. Krystal would never do something like that to Mackenzie or any other child!" he said.

"You don't know what happened in that room. You only know what that bitch told you!"

"Mackenzie said she fell also, and I heard Krystal telling her to stop jumping on the bed."

"What were they doing in there anyway? Mackenzie is your responsibility when she goes to your place, not your bitch!" I fumed.

"Don't you think I know that? I was taking a bath and they were watching TV in there. I think Mackenzie is acting out because of all the bullshit that you've been feeding her."

"Oh no! Don't you put that shit on me!"

"I'm gonna put it on you because if you hadn't told her all that crazy shit, we wouldn't have any problems with her. You are telling her to not listen to Krystal and how she's an evil witch out to steal her daddy from her. You're doing all of this for nothing Malayka!"

"The bottom line is if you can't keep your eyes on our daughter when she visits you, maybe I'm the one who needs to see a lawyer and ask for sole custody," I threatened.

"Wooooow! So that's what this shit is about?"

"What shit?"

"This whole charade you got going on. You just wanna strip me of my rights," he said.

"That's not true!"

"It is true, but guess what? It's not gonna be that easy. Mackenzie is my daughter too and I've been there from day one. I'm not going anywhere," he stated.

"It ain't about you Zion. It's about Mackenzie. She's only four years old and needs adult supervision!"

"She had adult supervision..."

"I can't tell. I'm just gonna take a picture of her forehead and keep it as documentation. You better hope this never happens again," I said as I hung the phone up in his face.

I knew that Zion was a good father, but with that bitch influencing him, who knew what the future held. I loved Zion, but if I had to keep him from his daughter to protect her, then so be it.

Eventually, he'd realize what was best for our daughter, and it wasn't his bitch!

CHAPTER TWELVE

Zion

Okay, I knew that Malayka wasn't going to be happy about the knot on Mackenzie's forehead, but that was an accident. It's true that I wasn't in the room when it happened, but I knew for a fact that Krystal never did anything to cause that to happen. I was sitting in the tub when I heard Krystal tell her a couple of times to stop jumping in the bed. By the time I got out of the tub, Mackenzie was screaming bloody murder and Krystal was running around like a chicken with her head cut off.

When she told me that Mackenzie fell off the bed, I had no doubt that she was telling the truth. Why wouldn't I believe it? Mackenzie was crying too much to say anything, but I believed Krystal. I wanted to call Malayka when it happened, but Krystal talked me out of it. She said that it didn't make any sense to worry Malayka when she could deal with Mackenzie. I watched her put ice on Mackenzie's swollen mound and she held it there for about half an hour. Thank God there was no broken skin. It was just a lump.

Once she took the ice pack off, she rubbed the wound with some petroleum jelly and we gave her some Tylenol. I read online that she needed to stay awake for two hours, so we watched TV with her until the two hours was up. She finally fell asleep, but I kept checking on her throughout the night to make sure she was okay. Now that Malayka was going off on me about it, I felt wrong for not letting her know what happened to Mackenzie on Saturday.

When I hung the phone up, Krystal was standing there looking at me with her arms over her chest. "Let me guess... she's blaming me for the accident. It's all my fault, huh?"

"Well, she's mad because we didn't tell her about it when it happened."

"What for? It's not like if she would've been able to prevent it from happening. It had already happened. What difference does it make when she found out?" Krystal asked.

"Well, Mackenzie is her daughter too, babe. I can see why she's pissed at me for not telling her sooner. I'd probably feel the same way if something happened to Mackenzie with her and she didn't let me know."

"But babe, she's making a big deal out of nothing. Mackenzie is fine, except for the lump on her head. That's gonna go away in a couple of days, I promise. Don't let her make you feel as if you did something wrong. You didn't!" Krystal said as she wrapped her arms around my waist. "You're a great father and anyone who knows you knows that about you. She's just bitter because she can't have you."

I knew that Krystal had a point. Malayka probably was still mad about our conversation two weeks ago when I told her I never loved her and was going to marry Krystal. I didn't know what kind of shit was running through Malayka's mind. I couldn't figure it out if I tried because she was such a spiteful person. I just hoped that things between the three of us got better for Mackenzie's sake. She didn't need three out of control adults trying to help mold her.

"I love you," Krystal said.

"Yea? How much?" I asked with a sly smile.

"Follow me and I'll show you," she said.

I did just that. I followed her to the bedroom and watched her remove all her clothes. She got down on her knees and dropped my pants, then pulled my dick out. She took it in her hands and stroked it as she sucked on my balls. My knees began to knock into each other as she wrapped her lips around my dick. She sucked my dick and got it sloppy wet for the next few minutes. When I felt weak kneed to the point where I couldn't stand anymore, I pulled her up and kissed her deeply.

She moved over to the bed and got on all fours. She looked back at me as I got behind her and began to lick her from front to back. I drove my tongue deep inside her and sucked all her juices. "Mmmmm!" she moaned.

When I removed my face from between her ass cheeks, I removed my shirt. She looked back at me and said, "I have a surprise for you."

"I love surprises," I said.

"Mmm hmm!" she said.

I got behind her and pushed my dick inside her wet pussy. As she arched her back, I pounded her insides. "Oh yea! Right there, baby!" she moaned. As I continued to pound her from behind, she looked back at me with a sexy expression on her face. "Mmm! Put your finger in my asshole, baby."

Oh wow! My baby had been watching some porn flicks if she wanted me to do that. I did as she asked, and her moans grew louder. I spit on her ass as I drove my finger inside while still fucking her pussy. "You like that?" I asked.

"Oh yes baby! It feels so good!" she cried. "I wanna feel it in my ass!"

"Wait, what?" I asked as I pulled out of her pussy.

"I want us to try something different," she said with a smile. She reached under the pillow and pulled out a bottle of KY Jelly. She handed me the bottle and watched me for a few minutes. I wasn't sure that I understood her correctly, so I hesitated. "What are you waiting for?"

"Because I'm not sure I understand what you want."

"Babe, it's simple. I want you to lubricate my ass and put your dick in it," she said with a laugh. I had never put my dick in a woman's asshole before, so I wasn't sure if I wanted to go there. I mean, of course I had seen it done before. I watched porn on Pornhub, so I had seen that done to women before. I just never thought I'd be asked to do it.

I had stood there with my mouth hung open for so long that my dick had lost it hardness. She looked at me with a disappointed look on her face. "Babe, what's wrong? Don't you want to try new things with me? I'm trying to keep the excitement in our sex life, so why are you standing there looking like I asked you to eat shit with me? If you can drive your tongue inside my ass, why can't you do the same thing with your dick?"

"It's not that I can't do it. It's just that I've never done that before," I said.

"So, you don't want to try something new with me?" She looked a little confused, but also a little hurt. I really didn't know what to do because she had really caught me off guard.

"I'm not saying that babe. I guess you just surprised me, ya know? You caught me a little off guard with your request."

"I'm sorry. I didn't mean to have you feeling some kind of way. I just thought we'd try something new, but I guess it's too soon."

"Yea, that might be what it is. I just feel like maybe somewhere down the line, we could try it, but not right now," I said. I didn't want to hurt her feelings or anything like that, but she had caught me by surprise so much that I didn't even wanna have sex anymore. I looked at my limp dick and grabbed my boxers off the floor and put them on.

"You don't wanna have sex anymore?" she asked looking disappointed.

"Babe, I'm not even hard anymore. Like that shit just shocked the hell out of me."

"Damn Zion! Can you live a little for once?"

"You could've warned me before you just sprung it on me..."

"Warned you?! It ain't even that serious!" she said angrily. "You know what? Never mind. Forget I asked you anything about trying something new. We'll just continue to fuck the same boring ass ways you're used to!"

She jumped out of bed and stormed out of the room. Her attitude really shocked me. I didn't know what had gotten into her. I wondered if someone had told her something that would make her think I needed her to do that. I wasn't saying that I was completely against the two of us doing it that way. She just shocked me by her request.

I got dressed and went to look for her. I didn't want her to be angry. I just wanted her to see things from my point of view. I found her in the living room crying on the sofa. I went to sit next to her, so we could talk it out. "Babe, I'm sorry. I don't want you to cry," I said.

"You just made me feel so cheap," she said.

"How? How did I do that?"

"You should've seen the look on your face when I made the suggestion. It was like I was some dirty slut or something!"

"Babe, I'm sorry if I made you feel like that. That wasn't my intention. I promise you that I was just shocked. I ain't ever done nothing like that before," I confessed.

"Yea, that was pretty obvious. I guess I just wanted to make sure that I keep you satisfied, especially in the bedroom. The last thing I want is for you to leave me for someone who is willing to try different things..."

"Hey, wait a minute. Where is this coming from? You know that I love you. I'm not even thinking about getting with anyone else."

"You promise?"

I pulled her closer to me. "Baby, I love you. You're all the woman I need."

"Please don't ever leave me," she said as she held me close.

"I'm not gonna leave you babe. I don't know what happened but get that out of your head."

"I guess it's because I know your baby mama is trying to break us up. She thinks I hurt your baby, doesn't she?"

"She never said..."

"Don't lie to me Zion. I heard you on the phone telling her that I'd never do that. I want you to know that I'd never hurt Mackenzie. I love her just as much as I love you."

"Babe, I know that. You'd never hurt Mackenzie. Malayka is just upset that we didn't tell her right away. She'll calm down in a few hours. You don't need to concern yourself about that," I said.

"Okay. Just know that I love you and I love Mackenzie with all my heart."

"I already know that baby. So, are we good?" I asked.

"We're good," she said as she leaned in and kissed me.

Thank God. The last thing in the world I wanted was to lose my woman behind some more bullshit with Malayka.

CHAPTER THIRTEEN

Krystal

The past few weeks with Zion had been great. We hadn't seen Mackenzie in almost a month and that was because her mom was feeling some kind of way about letting us have her. That was fine with me. The less we had to worry about her little brat, the better. I suspected that she was still pissed about Mackenzie falling off the bed. Shit, Mackenzie had been having little "accidents" every time she came over to our place. I was hoping she would get tired of the little marks and bruises and keep her kid with her.

When she told Zion she was keeping Mackenzie for his past two weekends, I was ecstatic. However, he didn't share my feelings. He was truly upset about missing time with his daughter. No matter what I did or said, he missed his little girl. Sometimes, he acted like such a bitch. His baby mama was the biggest bitch though.

I couldn't believe she was still holding a damn grudge because her little brat got hurt while she was visiting with her dad. So fucking what? She could still walk, run, and do whatever else her little spoiled ass wanted to do. She was still breathing normally without an oxygen tank. I mean, the way that bitch acted, you could've sworn her kid got hauled away in a body bag.

I knew that it was wrong of me to be using that child to get back at her mom. The way I felt about their situation was if the child wasn't around, Zion wouldn't have to deal with the mom anymore. I was so sick of her ass. I mean, for real.

The night Mackenzie got hurt Zion had asked me to watch her so he could take a shower. I agreed and asked Mackenzie if she wanted to watch TV in her room and she said yes.

I didn't plan for her to fall off the bed. However, I did know that if we went in her room, she'd be tempted to jump on her bed. We had been having trouble keeping her from doing that for the past few weeks. When she started jumping on the bed, I didn't even try to stop her. I mean, a lesson had to be learned in all of this. So, even though my mouth said the words, "Stop doing that Kenzie," my actions showed differently. I made hand gestures and gave head nods that let her think it was okay for her to jump in the bed. I even told her that it would be our little secret.

Shit, the only reason I even told her to stop was so it would look good in front of Zion. I knew that he could hear me telling her to quit jumping because I said it loud enough for him to hear me. I continued to encourage her to jump on the bed until I "accidentally" bumped her. When I did that, she flew off the bed and onto the floor. Oops! I immediately rushed to her aide, picked her up off the floor and apologized.

"I'm so sorry Kenzie. I didn't mean to bump you baby. Please don't say anything to your daddy, okay?" I asked. She was crying uncontrollably as I carried her to the kitchen to get an ice pack.

Zion came rushing into the kitchen when he heard her crying and almost shitted on himself when he saw the huge knot on her forehead. I think she bumped her head on the corner of her bed or something because she had carpet in her bedroom. She couldn't have hit it on the floor, but that's what I told Zion happened.

"What happened?" he asked.

"She fell off the bed and hit her head."

"Oh my God!" he said as he took her from my arms.

He took her to the living room sofa where she continued to cry. He took the ice pack from me and pressed it against her forehead. "I'm sorry babe. She was jumping on the bed and lost her footing. The next thing I knew, she went flying off the bed."

"Mackenzie, you know that you aren't supposed to be jumping on the bed baby. This is what happens when you do things you aren't supposed to. Now, you have a huge bump on your head," he said. As he looked at the swelling on her forehead, I saw the worried look on his face. "I think I should call Malayka and let her know what happened."

"What... why?"

"Look at her forehead babe. She might need her mom to take her to the hospital."

"Zion if it were that bad, I'd suggest that we take her. It isn't that bad. The skin hasn't even broken," I reasoned. "All you have to do is keep the ice pack on her head for a little while longer. After you're done with that, I'll put some Vaseline on it and then give her some Tylenol. She'll be fine in a couple of days."

"Are you sure?" he asked.

"Duh! You think I'd be telling you all that if I wasn't sure?"

"I hope you're right."

Mackenzie finally stopped crying, but he kept the ice pack on her head. "I want mommy," Mackenzie cried.

"Aww, I thought you wanted to stay with daddy and KK, so we could have some fun," I said.

Of course, I couldn't care less at this point if she went home to that bitch. I just didn't want her to leave right now. I had a feeling that if she went home with that knot on her forehead tonight, her mom wouldn't hesitate to call the police to try and press charges. That was the last thing we needed was to be accused of some kind of child abuse.

"I just want my mommy," the brat whined.

"Hand me my phone," Zion said to me.

"No. This is your weekend. She only has to stay one more day and tomorrow she'll be back home with her mom."

"But I have a feeling that Malayka is going to shit when she sees her forehead."

"I'm sure she will. That bitch..." I stopped midsentence because I promised Zion that I wouldn't criticize that heifa in front of his little brat. Sometimes, I wondered if messing with Zion was even worth it, but then I thought about the bigger picture. He had a great job and made great money. He had already moved me into his house and we had even talked about getting married.

Once we got married, I was going to get pregnant and made sure that he'd forget all about the first kid he had with that bitch. "I'm sorry. I just know that she's always blaming us for something and this time is going to be no different."

"You're right. Sweetie, we're gonna take care of you tonight and then tomorrow, I'll bring you back to your mom's. Okay?" Zion asked.

I couldn't believe how much they spoiled this kid. I mean, he was asking her if it was okay if she stayed over tonight and he'd bring her back tomorrow. What the fuck? When I was growing up, what my parents said was what went. They didn't care if I was cool with it or not.

"Okay," she said. I stood up and went to get the Tylenol. I gave her a teaspoon in a medicinal measuring cup. She drank it and two hours later, Zion tucked her in and we went to bed. I wasn't worried about the bitch and how she would feel tomorrow. I just hoped she'd decide to keep her brat with her from here on out. That's what I was aiming for anyway.

When Mackenzie wasn't here, my relationship with Zion was totally different. I was more relaxed and felt like this was my home. I was able to just chill with my man and be myself. When his daughter was around, I felt tense all the time and I knew that was because her mom would be calling to check on her. I cringed every time the phone rang, and it was Malayka.

So, this weekend she was finally allowing Zion to have Mackenzie again. Ugh! To say that I was pissed would be an understatement. The past month with Zion had been fantastic. We had even gone out of town a couple of times. I knew he missed his baby, but if all went well, he wouldn't have to worry about her anymore.

Zion was picking Mackenzie up from daycare and bringing her home. She'd be going back to her mom's house Sunday.

I wasn't looking forward to that, but okay. I just had to show Zion how good things were between us when his daughter wasn't here. He needed to see that our lives were better without his little spoiled brat. When they walked in the door, I was taking the fries out of the pot. I had decided to make a simple meal of cheeseburgers and French fries for dinner.

"Hi Kenzie!" I shrieked as if I was happy to see her.

"Hi KK, what are you doing?" she asked as she joined me in the kitchen.

"About to put these burgers together, so we could eat dinner."

"Oh, I love cheeseburgers!" she said excitedly.

"I know, that's why I made them. Why don't you and your dad go wash up and by the time y'all are done, the food will be on the table."

"Okay," she said as she rushed to the bathroom. Zion gave me a kiss on the lips and hugged me tight.

"What was that for?" I asked.

"For making cheeseburgers and fries. You know how much she loves them," he said.

"Yea, I know. You better go help her before she floods the bathroom."

"You're right." He hurriedly made his way down the hallway as I prepared the food. I placed the plates on the table with some glasses of fruit punch Kool-aid and waited for the two of them to join me. They walked back into the dining room laughing about whatever.

The next couple of days went by smoothly until Sunday. We were out in the backyard enjoying the beautiful afternoon. Zion was pushing Mackenzie on the swing set he had put together for her a couple of years ago when he suddenly had to go to the bathroom. Mackenzie didn't want to stop swinging, so Zion asked me if I could continue to push her until he came back out.

"Sure," I said with a smile. I stood up from my comfortable spot on the chaise lounge and walked over to where the swing set was.

"I'll be right back," Zion said as he rushed inside the house.

"Push me KK!" Mackenzie said.

I began to push her even though I didn't want to. "HIGHER!" she shouted.

I pushed her harder and she went higher. She squealed in delight as she went higher and higher. When she came back down for me to push her again, I roughly grabbed the chain link of the swing and she fell flat on the ground, her face buried in the dirt. She didn't start crying right away, so I was worried that the fall had killed her. When she removed her face from the dirt, she screamed so loud, I knew she could be heard a block over. I didn't notice the angle her arm was in at first until I tried to move her.

When I tried to move her, she screamed louder than before, causing Zion to burst through the door that led to the backyard. "Oh God! What happened?" he asked in a hasty tone.

"I don't know. I was just pushing her on the swing, she asked to go higher, and then she just fell!" I cried.

I watched as he tried to move her, but she screamed in pain when he tried to pick her up. "Oh my God! I think her arm is broken!" he cried.

"What?! How could her arm be broken? She wasn't even that high up when she fell!"

"I don't know, but I need to find a way to stabilize her arm, so I can bring her to the hospital!"

"You really think her arm is broken?" I asked.

"Uh, do you not see the bone sticking out on the inside of her skin?" he asked as he rushed inside the house. Mackenzie continued to shriek as we waited for Zion to come back. He returned with a piece of rag that looked like a ripped up t-shirt. He put it around Mackenzie's arm then tied it around her neck. The whole entire time, she continued to scream bloody murder.

As he slowly picked her up, I followed behind him. Now, I know y'all probably think I'm a bitch right about now, but I never meant for that child to break her little arm. I know that was a chance that I was taking, but that was really an accident. I thought she'd skin her chin or her knees, but I certainly didn't think she'd break an arm.

I grabbed the keys and opened the back door of Zion's truck, so he could climb in with Mackenzie. I shut the door and climbed into the driver's seat. A couple of minutes later, I heard him making a phone call. I already knew who he was calling before he said anything. When he ended the call, I looked in the rearview mirror at him.

"What'd she say?" I asked.

"Just watch the road please," he said.

We pulled into the emergency room area a short time later and Zion rushed in. I parked the truck and went to find him. Before I walked in the hospital, I said a prayer that I wouldn't have to hurt Zion or his baby mama today. "Lord, please keep these people safe because if either of them get outta line with me, I'ma have to put these hands on them. Now, you know as well as I do that I never meant to hurt that child that bad. Shit just happened. But I'ma need you to standby because I have a feeling that the worse is yet to come." I made my sign of the cross and went inside.

I was led to the room where Zion was with Mackenzie and a nurse. 15 minutes later, I was being asked to leave by that bitch. As I paced the waiting room, I really wanted to put my hands on her. How dare she speak to me that way? How could Zion let her talk to me like that? He was supposed to get in her ass for disrespecting me, but he didn't.

We were definitely going to have a talk about that shit...

CHAPTER FOURTEEN

Zion

I didn't know what happened outside when Krystal was pushing Mackenzie. All I knew was I was taking a shit and I heard my child screaming so loud, I had to cut the shit short. I jumped off the toilet, barely wiping my ass or washing my hands, and rushed outside to find my four-year old face down on the ground. Krystal was kneeling beside her with a worried look on her face. I tried to move my baby, but she started screaming louder. That was when I realized that her arm was broken. I quickly ran in the house, trying to fight back my tears.

I needed something to use as a sling to get my baby to the hospital. I tore one of my t-shirts because I didn't have the time to keep looking. I tied it around Mackenzie's neck after getting her arm inside it and slowly picked her up off the ground. As Krystal and I rushed to the truck, I waited for her to lock the house up, so she could open the back door. She opened the door and I slid inside while holding my screaming daughter in my arms. Calling Malayka was the hardest thing I had to do because I just knew that she was going to literally have a cow.

Just as I suspected, she was screaming at me through the phone receiver.

"Hey Zion, what's..." She answered the phone, but she never got to finish her question. I guess she heard Mackenzie screaming and her motherly instincts went in full speed. "What's going on? Why is Mackenzie screaming like that?"

"We're on our way to Texas Children's Hospital. Can you meet us there?" I asked.

"Texas Children's? What happened to my baby?" There was no way in hell I was going to tell this woman what happened to our daughter over the phone. She was just gonna have to meet me at the hospital and then I'd give her the information.

"I'll explain everything when you get there! I have to go!" With that, I quickly ended the call. As I tried to soothe Mackenzie, she continued to scream. Her little screams were starting to take on a hoarse effect and her face was red and puffy like her eyes. I wished I could take away her pain, but there was no way that I could do that, no matter how much I wanted to.

Krystal pulled up to the emergency room doors and opened the back door for me. I slid out and rushed inside with my baby girl. The nurses immediately began to tend to her, asking me all kinds of questions about what happened. I didn't know how to answer because I didn't see what happened. I just told them she fell off her swing. Krystal joined me a short time later, but when Malayka burst through the door, all hell broke loose.

I thought she was going to beat Krystal's ass right there in the room with the doctor present. She had given Mackenzie a pain killer which she said would make her sleep, so they could take the x-rays of her arm. She said that she knew Mackenzie's arm was broken from looking at it, but needed to do x-rays to find out where and how it was broken. I had to send Krystal out to the waiting room though to keep the two women from fighting.

Once Krystal had left the room, Malayka turned to the doctor. "Did you give my four year old a sedative?"

"No ma'am. I gave her something for pain," the doctor said. "As I was telling your husband before you walked in, your daughter's arm is broken. I need to get an x-ray done to find out where it's broken and how I can fix it. Once the x-ray is complete, I'm going to take her down to the operating room and perform the surgery to repair the broken arm."

"So, my daughter's arm is broken?" Malayka asked.

"Yes ma'am, but don't worry. I can fix it."

She turned to me with tears in her eyes. "How did this happen?"

"She fell off her swing," I said.

"She fell off her swing? How hard were you pushing her Zion? How hard were you pushing her to make her fall off the swing and break her damn arm?" she asked.

Now, as much as I loved Krystal, I had to tell the truth. I couldn't have Malayka looking at me as if I was irresponsible and shit. I wasn't responsible for our daughter being laid up in this damn hospital bed.

"Actually, Krystal was pushing her..."

"KRYSTAL? Krystal did this to my baby?" I asked.

"It was an accid..." I didn't get to finish my statement before Malayka rushed out the room. "I'll be right back doctor. Please do what you need to do to get the surgery done." I flew out of the room and ran down the hallway. I could see Malayka walking fast as hell as I tried to catch up to her.

She pushed the doors to the lobby open and I couldn't say what happened next because by the time I got out to the waiting room, the two women were in a full fledge fist fight. There were a couple of people recording on their phones and I heard a nurse call for security. I pulled Malayka off of Krystal and someone else held Krystal back.

"LET GO OF ME ZION!!" Malayka yelled.

"No! Our daughter needs you right now! How do you think she's gonna feel when she wakes up and you're not here because you got arrested?" I asked her.

"What the hell is that bitch's problem anyway?" Krystal asked.

"You know exactly what my problem is bitch! You are the reason my daughter is laid up in that hospital bed! You're the reason she has to undergo surgery to repair her broken arm! I told Zion that you were a no good bitch, so to find out you've been abusing my daughter!!"

"ABUSING?! I AIN'T DID SHIT TO MACKENZIE!" Krystal yelled.

"Oh bitch! You better watch yourself from here on out!" Malayka said.

"Are you threatening me?" Krystal asked.

"HELL NO BITCH! I'M MAKING YOU A GOTDAMN PROMISE!" Malayka said as she jerked her arm from my grasp. "Let go of me!"

She mean mugged Krystal and pointed to her as she retreated to the back to be with our daughter. Krystal stood there looking at me with a black eye and busted lip. For someone who had just accused Malayka of not being able to fight, she sure looked like she got her ass whooped. "You're just gonna let her talk to me like that?" Krystal asked.

"I can't deal with this shit right now. Mackenzie has to have surgery and I have to be there when she wakes up. Why don't you go home, and I'll call you when she comes out of surgery?" I asked.

"Why can't I wait for you here?"

"Because I don't know how long the surgery is gonna last and you don't need to sit out here by yourself."

"Well, you could come sit out here with me."

"I can't. I have to be back there to support Malayka..."

"It's always Malayka! You're always worried about her more than me!" she whined.

"I'm not gonna do this now Krystal. Go home!" I said as I turned my back and walked through the double doors that would take me back to where Mackenzie and Malayka were.

"ZION! ZION!" Krystal screamed after me, but I continued to walk. This was in no way, shape or form about her. I wasn't going to let her make this about her right now. It was about Mackenzie and she was the only one that mattered right about now.

I walked back to the room to find Malayka fixing her hair in the mirror. "You alright?"

"I'm fine."

"Where's Mackenzie?"

"They came get her to bring her to get the x-rays done. She shouldn't be too much longer."

"I'm sorry," I said.

"Sorry? About what?" she asked as she stared at me in the mirror.

"I'm sorry this shit happened. I never meant for any of this to happen."

"Yea, well, we'll talk about it once I get my baby home. You can believe that shit!"

"Oh, I do."

We sat quietly and waited for the x-ray tech to bring Mackenzie back. There wasn't anything that needed to be said at this point. I knew that nothing I said to Malayka would erase what happened to Mackenzie. No matter how many times I apologized, nothing would get solved.

The quiet time did give me some time to think and reflect though. That was twice our baby got hurt and both times was when she was with Krystal. I didn't think that she had purposely done anything to hurt Mackenzie, but I knew that she hadn't been watching her properly. I knew that Malayka was going to take her sweet time sending Mackenzie back to my house again. I couldn't say that I blamed her though.

First, our daughter ended up with a big ass knot on her forehead. This time, she has a broken arm. Yea, if shit like that was going on at Malayka's crib, I'd do the exact same thing. I was definitely going to have a serious talk with Krystal about this because shit like this could never happen again.

My daughter was too precious and too fragile to be getting hurt this way. I just hoped that Krystal hadn't done any of this on purpose because Lord help her if she did.

CHAPTER FIFTEEN

Malayka

Once Krystal left the room, I turned to Zion and said, "You let this shit happen."

"What do you mean by that? I didn't do anything to Mackenzie!"

"I told you since the bump on the head that your bitch had done it. And I could bet any money that she's responsible for this too!" I said as I pointed in his face.

"Ssshh! You don't want this doctor getting the wrong idea!" he said through clenched teeth as he looked around me at the doctor.

"I don't give a fuck who thinks what about your bitch!"

Watching my baby suffer with a broken arm was something that hurt me to the core. I could literally feel the pain etched in my heart because of it. I loved my little girl with all of my being. The one thing in this world I'd never tolerate was someone putting their hands on her. The doctor said she could fix her broken arm, but the fact that she had to go through that nearly tore me to pieces. I could barely see as the tears formed in my eyes.

"How did this happen?" I asked as I turned my attention back to Zion.

"She fell off her swing."

"She fell off her swing? Damn Zion, how hard were you pushing her? I mean seriously... how hard were you pushing her to make her fall off the swing and break her damn arm?" I was absolutely livid, and I hope he knew that there was no answer that he could give me that wouldn't make me fly off the handle. As a mother, whatever pain my baby felt, I felt. It was different for moms than dads because we carried our babies under our hearts for nine months, sometimes longer.

We were the ones our babies looked to when they were in pain. I'd put my last dollar on the fact that when this happened, Mackenzie was crying for me.

Knowing that fact had me seeing red. Not just any red either. The same red that would make a bull charge a matador. That kind of red.

"Uuhhhh, actually, Krystal was pushing her..."

"KRYSTAL? Krystal did this to my baby?" I asked. Just having him confirm what I already knew made my insides boil like a hot water heater. I knew all along that the bitch didn't like me, and trust me, the feeling was fucking mutual. But to take her frustrations out on my innocent child... that was something that was unacceptable. She was going to pay for this shit.

Hearing those words flow from Zion's lips...

When he said that Krystal had been pushing Mackenzie on the swing, I knew this was done on purpose. She had hurt my baby girl in order to hurt me. I couldn't believe I had trusted Zion to keep an eye on our daughter while that bitch was around. For the past three to four months, I had been noticing little bruises here and there on Mackenzie's body. Every time I asked her about it, she just said she fell, or she didn't remember. When I mentioned the shit to Zion, he always said that she fell or bumped herself.

Now, I knew that sometimes kids had accidents, but the type of shit that was going on with my little girl would make her a fucking klutz. Now, if she was so accident prone when she was with her father, surely, she'd exhibit the same functionality when she was with me, right? I wasn't trying to just make shit up because I didn't like that bitch. I was really concerned about my little girl.

I was starting to think that Zion didn't know what the hell was going on with our child, but I wasn't stupid. I had been taking pictures and keeping a record of every single incident my child had while she was in her dad's care. I was going to use it if I ever had to take his ass to court because he wasn't protecting her the way he should've been. I had something written down every single time she came back from his place, even if she had so much as a hair out of place.

"Malayka, it was an accid..."

I didn't even wait for him to finish his statement. I was sick and tired of him covering for that low-down, dirty bitch. This incident here was the final fucking straw. My child wasn't going back to Zion's place, not as long as that bitch was living there. When he said Krystal was the one pushing Mackenzie on the swing, I immediately left the exam room. I flew out of that door like bats out of a bat cave imploded with fireworks. I practically sprinted my way to the waiting room to confront that bitch. When I burst through the doors, I didn't say shit, at first. I spotted her sitting in a chair by the window, walked up to her, and slapped the shit out of her.

"What the fuck..."

She didn't have a chance to say anything else as I slapped her again, this time with more force than the last time. That was when she swung back at me and the fight was on. I wasn't thinking about getting arrested or the fact that we were actually fighting in a hospital waiting room. The only thing that I was thinking about was my baby girl and her broken arm. That bitch said I couldn't fight earlier, but I was about to prove her wrong. It's amazing the strength a mother can have when it came to protecting her child.

I was like a lioness when she tried to protect her cub from harm. The fear in my child's eyes before she fell asleep was what gave me the strength I needed to bust this bitch's fucking ass. I punched, slapped, and pulled her fucking hair like it was her own. If I could've yanked that shit from her fucking scalp, I would've. Some kind of way, I managed to climb on top of her and just started punching her in her damn face.

"YOU DID THAT TO MY DAUGHTER!" I said as I punched her hard in the eye. "YOU'RE THE REASON SHE'S HERE!"

WHAP!

"You will never ever get another chance to put your hands on my baby again!"

WHAP!

I punched her one last time before Zion pulled me off of her. My heart was beating so fast, I thought it was going to bounce right up outta my chest. I wanted to punch the shit out of Zion too, but there would be plenty of time for that later. Right now, my concern was for my little girl. I took deep breaths to try and get my breathing back to normal.

"If I find out that you purposely had anything to do with my daughter lying in that hospital bed, I'm pressing charges on your ass. And that's after I fuck you up again bitch!" I said as I jerked my arm from Zion's grasp and made my way back through the double doors.

I had never been in a fight like that before in my life. Well, that isn't completely true. I had a couple of fights in high school, but they were playdates compared to today's fight. That was one of those knock-down, drag out kinda fights. That bitch had another thing coming if she thought that I was going to let that shit slide. She may have Zion's ass fooled, but not me. I knew from the jump that she was a triflin' bitch. I made it to the exam room as the doctor was looking at Mackenzie's x-rays.

"What happened to you?" she asked me.

"Don't worry about me doctor. How's my baby?"

"She's still under sedation."

I used the back of my hand to dab at the blood that was dripping from a cut on my face. The doctor handed me a tissue. "Thank you. What are you going to do for my baby?" I asked as I stared at the x-rays with her.

"Well, as you can see, her arm is fractured here. What I'm gonna do is give her a mild anesthetic and fix the broken bone," she said.

"How long is that gonna take?"

"The surgery itself should take a couple of hours. She'll need to wear a cast for two to three months, but once it's removed, she'll be as good as new."

"Thanks doc," I said.

By the time Zion returned, they had taken Mackenzie to the operating room. I had cleaned my face and was in the process of fixing my hair when he walked in.

"Are you alright?" he asked.

"If you know what's good for you, you'll keep your trap shut right about now," I said.

"Where's Mackenzie?"

"Where the fuck do you think she is? In surgery ASS!"

"Malay..."

"Don't fuckin' talk to me Zion. Fa real!" I said through clenched teeth as I rolled my eyes at him.

For the next hour, we sat quietly in that room. Thoughts were roaming through my mind about how I should've protected my child better. All of a sudden, a rush of anger washed over me, and I set my sights on Zion. He was supposed to be Mackenzie's king, her protector. He was supposed to keep her safe when I wasn't there, but he didn't. I stood up slowly and walked over to where he was sitting. I hauled back as far as I could and did what I should've done the past few months.

WHAP!

I slapped him hard across the left side of his face. He grabbed his cheek and asked, "What was that for?"

"Because of you our baby is in surgery! Our four-year old is having surgery! I've never had a surgery in my whole damn life, but our little girl is having surgery!"

"Malayka..."

I raised my hand to shut him up. I didn't need, and I certainly didn't want to hear any of his excuses. And so help him if he tried to defend that bitch to me again. He was responsible for everything that was happening. Because I trusted him to keep our daughter safe, she was now having surgery. I trusted him and what's more important, Mackenzie trusted him. But he failed... he failed both of us.

"When my daughter was born, I took one look at her and made a promise to always keep her safe. I didn't do a good job before, but I can promise you that's going to change. I'm going to make that promise to her again and this time, I'm going to keep it... even if that means keeping you out of her life..."

"Wait... what?"

"You didn't keep our daughter safe Zion. You have been allowing that bitch to abuse our daughter for months. You never stepped in or tried to stop her, nothing. For that reason, I'm filing for sole custody of Mackenzie!"

"What? You're trying to take my daughter from me?" he asked with an incredulous look plastered on his face. A face I once thought was so handsome, but now I couldn't stand to look at. How had things between us gotten to this point? To a point where I couldn't trust my daughter with him?

"No, but I am going to request that you have supervised visitation," I said.

"Supervised visitation? Malayka, you're being unreasonable..."

"Unreasonable? Nigga you got me fucked up if you think that! I gave you chance after chance to get control over that bitch. I told you about Mackenzie's bruises and what did you do? Nothing. Not a damn thang! You put her life in jeopardy! You put her in harm's way and that is the reason we are sitting here right now WHILE OUR DAUGHTER IS GETTING OPERATED ON!" I screamed.

"Malayka, you can't do that! I'm a good father..."

"You used to be. Lately, you've made everything about you and your whore instead of our baby girl. I trusted you, but I won't make that mistake again," I said.

And I meant that shit from the bottom of my heart and the depths of my soul. Mackenzie is a baby who couldn't protect herself from the evil of that bitch, but I could. As long as she had me in her corner, she never had to worry about anyone hurting her ever again. She was my main priority and she came first, no ifs, ands, or buts about it!

They fucked with the wrong one, but they got the right one today!!

To be continued...

CPSIA information can be obtained
at www.ICGtesting.com
Printed in the USA
LVHW091831071218
599658LV00005B/551/P